The Last Lord's Wife

Written by
E.C. Pieterse

America Star Books

© 2014 by America Star Books.
All rights reserved. No part of this book may be reproduced, stored in a retrieval system or transmitted in any form or by any means without the prior written permission of the publishers, except by a reviewer who may quote brief passages in a review to be printed in a newspaper, magazine or journal.

First printing

All characters in this book are fictitious, and any resemblance to real persons, living or dead, is coincidental.

America Star Books has allowed this work to remain exactly as the author intended, verbatim, without editorial input.

Corrector: M.M. McHugh
Illustrator front: N.J.A. Koeken

Softcover 9781611024838
PUBLISHED BY AMERICA STAR BOOKS, LLLP
www.americastarbooks.com

Printed in the United States of America

For Nat,

For being the shoulder I lean on,
The ear that listens,
The foot that kicks my butt when I'm my own worst enemy,
And the best friend a girl could ask for.

For Mom,

For threatening to break into my house if I didn't take a chance on this soon.

Thank you Monica for the editing this second version.

Table of Contents

1. Meetings 7
2. Preparations 14
3. Travels 19
4. Feelings 25
5. Injury 31
6. Wandering 38
7. Confusion 45
8. Ambush 49
9. Disagreement 59
10. Visitors 66
11. Disclosures 74
12. Consequences 84
13. Storm 91
14. Shelter 96
15. Reveal 101
16. Chances 110
17. Acquaintances 116
18. Accident 123
19. Apprehension 129
20. Surprise 138
21. Advice 144
22. Amends 152

23. Ordeal	161
24. Confrontation	170
25. Conclusion	179
26. Arrival	187
27. Journey	195
28. Trepidation	207
29. Aid	216
30. Finale	226

1
Meetings

She never felt that special, even if people around her claimed her to be. She saw herself for what she was; a motherless child, raised by her father and his second wife, her aunt.

A motherless child since the age of three. She had watched her mother die after being stabbed in the chest by a dagger. Who had done it? The child did not know, and neither did the young woman who had replaced that child. It was partly why people thought she was special.

The other reason was because she was the only daughter of Lord Frederick Gaeli of Geastwood Castle, the only child of Lady Lilliane. Two brothers had followed after her mother's death. Her aunt Louisa had been her mother's younger sister. They were alike; in manners and in appearance, but not in personalities. Where her mother had been kind and gentle, Lady Louisa was cold and difficult. She had no affection for the child that was not hers and very little for the two that were. Not even for the one that bore the same name as her sister; Lilliane Mariah Gaeli.

Her brothers. Only eleven and twelve years old, Frederick and Donovan had been training to become master swordsmen since they could walk. Donovan was intended to become the Lord of the Castle after their father had perished, Frederick a high ranking officer in the King's army. Both men were destined for glory and a life of honour. Her future was less predictable.

Turning fifteen in two days time meant her father's time of finding her a suitable husband was running out. If she was not married before her sixteenth birthday, there was little chance of her marrying afterwards. Young men of her age were scarce in this region. With the ongoing war, they did not have a long life expectancy either.

Sighing, she turned back to the task at hand. It was time to pack her things for the journey. Her lady's maid was waiting for her. Eliza was two years younger than she was. Her mother Beth had been her nurse, and indispensable after her own mother had passed.

Her father was sending her away to a convent three hundred miles upriver. Donovan was to escort her there. The convent was located in the capital, and much larger than the small village surrounding Geastwood Castle. Chances of finding a suitable husband were better.

Dinnertime was as usual a bustle of noise and people. Servants walked in and out of the room and her father was loudly entertaining guests. Sometimes they were clergymen or high trained officers from the village, other times they were noblemen travelling past them.

Lily was anxious. Surely her father would not send her to travel with only Donovan and her lady's maid at her side, yet he had not mentioned anyone else. To travel in wartime was dangerous enough, but her brother, no matter how skilled he was with his sword, was only twelve. Not a grown man yet. She knew her father cared very little for her as a daughter; he never had much time for her. Lord Frederick had a castle to run, messages to write to the King and two sons to educate. Daughters were the concern of his wife, but to let her travel alone with just a young lad at her side, it would not stand right with the other noblemen.

Yet it was not the only reason she was anxious. Eliza had taken her time with her chores today and this time she had driven it so far that she had made her mistress late for dinner.

She was almost five minutes late for the last dinner she would have with her family for a long time. She hastened along the corridors, Eliza following in her tracks. At least she had dressed for dinner earlier, while Eliza had packed. The door to the great hall was in sight. She stopped and after telling Eliza to go, took a deep breath before opening the doors. Normally a servant would open the door, but during dinner that servant was serving. Her hopes on entering unnoticed vanished when she saw all heads turning to the door. Her aunt was looking at her disapprovingly; her father on the other hand was smiling and stretching out his hand.

'And there she is, gentlemen, may I present to you my daughter, Lady Lilliane Gaeli of Geastwood Castle. Lilliane, these three men are high ranking officers in the King's army. They have agreed to travel with Donovan and you to St. Catherine's Convent.'

Her father grabbed her hand and patted it as he introduced the three men; James Johansson, a Lt. Marsh and Sir William Roderick Marsh. She nodded a welcome at the first two men, but Sir Marsh was out of her line of vision.

Lily quickly took her seat between her aunt and her youngest brother Frederick. They had already started eating soup; hers had been placed there and was almost entirely cold. She grabbed her spoon and pretended to eat, consciously aware of eyes studying her from across the table.

'What kept you?' hissed her aunt next to her.

'I am sorry Mother, I lost track of time.'

Mother; the word was spoken with the usual manner of respect, but not with love. She had no love for the woman that married her father three weeks after her mother's death. Not even as her aunt.

Her father signalled the servants to remove the soup and bring in the meat and bread. Lily happily let the servant remove the cold dish. Glancing upwards under her lashes, she dared to look at the man across the table. He had barely stopped staring at her since sitting down. Deep blue eyes locked with her brown ones, and a smirk that Lily felt belonged on his handsome face covered his lips. She nodded a hello at him then looked away, well aware of her aunt's presence next to her and what it would mean if she was caught staring at a man she had just met. She could feel him look away as well and sighed in half-relief.

As dinner progressed Lily listened to the men talk, occasionally answering a question if it was directed at her. She could feel eyes on her from time to time and knew that he was still looking at her. She didn't dare glance again, her aunt was keeping track of her every move.

Whoever this Sir William Roderick Marsh was, it might prove interesting to find out more about him.

It had seemed like a longer dinner than usual. Lily was glad when it was over and she could retire to her own chambers. The piercing blue eyes of Sir Marsh would follow her wherever she went in the room. She wondered why he found her so interesting; he had not said one word to her. As she turned around in her bed, she wondered what he was doing right now. Was he sound asleep, not a care in the world about the upcoming travels or was he awake, thinking about things...? Maybe even about her.

The Last Lord's Wife

She turned the other way, chastising herself for her thoughts. Although her father was a Christian and her mother had not been, she had been raised believing that thoughts about a man were wrong, especially the thoughts she was having. Sighing, she rose from her bed and pulled on her dressing gown. Perhaps a stroll in the moonlit corridors would do her some good; it always did when she was a child. And she could not be sure if she would ever truly be an inhabitant of the castle again.

She walked softly, staying out of the brightly lid parts of the hallways. Though she was known for nightly strolls it was frowned upon by her aunt. She was amazed that the light in the great hall was still on, laughter and singing could be heard coming her way as the wind blew through the open windows and into the corners of the old castle. She imagined Sir Marsh there, talking with her father, drinking wine and maybe even flirting with one of the servant girls. She quickly shook her head. The image made her frown, yet it also gave her the idea of a lifetime; this was the perfect moment to find out more about him. His quarters were nearby and all the men were downstairs. She shiftily walked towards his chambers, putting her ear to the door. No sound came from within, a sure sign that he was downstairs with the others. She opened the door and slipped inside.

She had been in these chambers before; a young lady had travelled with her father and they ate and rested at the castle. They looked different filled with male things. He had only been there since that afternoon, yet he had left his distinctive mark in every corner. Clothes and belongings covered the bed and some of the chairs. She appeared to be the only one there.

Slowly she moved her hands over the garments, feeling the soft fabric between her fingers, at the same time imagining how his skin would feel. No other man had ever made her feel this way. She wondered if he had even noticed it, or was she just some girl he was meant to transport? Would he really flirt with the servants? Some men were ruthless. She had seen it many times.

'This is a dangerous thing to do Milady.'

She turned suddenly at the sound of his voice. He was standing at a small distance from her, smirking at her with that peculiar grin of his. At first she looked at her feet, unsure what to respond to him, but when she saw he was dressed in nothing more than a cloth clinging to his waist, she quickly lifted her chin up in the air. His chest and legs were glistening with water drops and it took a moment for her to control herself. She had never seen a man looking like this before.

'Forgive me Sir; I must have taken a wrong turn.' She moved to pass him, but he grabbed her arm and stopped her.

'Did you now?'

'Yes. If you will excuse me, I must return to my own chambers.'

His grasp loosened, but he did not release her arm. 'Perhaps I should escort you back, to make sure you don't get lost again.'

'I fear that will make a wrong impression if anyone would spot us Sir, dressed in the attire you have on right now, especially at this hour of night,' she said boldly looking at his chest and bare legs.

It was his turn to look away. She was glad to see she had some effect on him as well.

'Your loose tongue will get you into trouble one day Lady Lilliane.'

He released her arm, grabbing his shirt from close by to pull it on. As he dropped the cloth that had been covering his rear and backside, she looked away wide eyed, unsure of what to do now. Should she leave immediately or wait until he dismissed her. He was slowly dressing himself, almost as if he was used to doing that with strange women in the room.

He finished and turned, surprised to still see her standing there.

'You are right Lady Lilliane, you should go.'

Though she was confused about his sudden brisk manner, she thought it best to obey this time. He was right after all; if one of her brothers caught her here, he was sure to tell their father and that would only lead to trouble. For her and for the man whose chambers she was currently in. Not to mention what would happen if her aunt caught her here.

As she slipped out of the room and crept towards her chambers, she realised how her excuse must have sounded to him. As if she could really take a wrong turn in the castle she had grown up in.

2

Preparations

The day began at dawn. Lily was awoken by a sleepy looking Eliza. She had not slept well. Her dreams were filled with Sir Marsh, her mother and aunt were there as well.

In one particular dream her mother had been walking around with a blood-soaked garment. Though her mouth was open, no sound could be heard. Her aunt seemed to be hiding in every corner. She had even tripped over her. Yet whenever she saw the glistening chest of William Marsh before her, the feelings of dread her mother and aunt were emanating could not touch her. She almost felt at peace.

Never the less the dreams had been so vivid that her mind had not rested. She had awoken a few times during the night as well.

Eliza chattered about the upcoming journey as she helped her dress. Lilliane said very little in reply, her own thoughts consumed her almost entirely.

At breakfast she feared to look at William Marsh, but neither he nor his brother were there. Mr Johansson told them they were scouting out the area and would return shortly. How would she act around him? She was determined to pretend that nothing had happened the night before; that no dreams had come to mind. Perhaps her mother had tried to warn her about him; she had attempted very hard to tell her something.

After breakfast Lilliane went down to the stables to saddle her mare Rose. Though it was something the stable boy Jack normally did, she wanted to do it herself today, or at least help. Rose had never been this far away from the castle either.

She entered the stables and stopped in the doorway; Sir Marsh was crouched near his horse. It had clearly been brushed and was now being prepared for their travels. She was surprised to see him here; surely it was not in his habit to take care of his own horse. A man of his stature didn't trouble himself with trivial things like that. Her father never did. Before she could contemplate on whether to move forward or back out before he saw her, she was met by the boy that worked in the stables.

'Ah, Lady Lilliane. I had a feeling you would be coming. Rose is just around the corner. She is almost ready for your journey. Eliza just gave me the last of your baggage to secure.'

Lily looked at the boy and smiled. 'Thank you Jack. I know you take exceptional care of our horses. Your father has trained you well.'

The boy smiled and bowed. He took up a canvas bag and walked further into the stables, bowing his head towards Sir Marsh as he passed him, and then rounded the corner.

Lily took a deep breath and prepared herself to follow Jack. Rose had been her goal of coming here after all. She passed Sir Marsh without acknowledging him and was almost sure he was doing the same until she felt his eyes burn on her back.

'Who is Rose?' he said in almost a whisper.

She debated on whether or not to turn and answer, but realised this man had done her no wrong; he deserved her best manners. Turning to him, she gestured her hand to where Jack had disappeared. 'Rose is my mare, I will be riding her.'

Sir Marsh focused on his horse again. Thinking this was the end of the conversation, Lilliane prepared to resume her path.

'You can't take her with you.'

'I beg your pardon?'

He fixed on her face. 'Your father is lending us a carriage for you and your lady's maid. Your horse will be in the way.'

'No, she will not. I don't need a carriage; I can ride Rose and Eliza can ride Dolly. A carriage will slow us down considerably.'

Sir Marsh did not reply, he held her stare, hardly blinking. His facial expression was one she could not read. She felt unnerved by his intent look, but did not back down. Finally he blinked and looked away.

'We leave in an hour, make sure you are ready, you and your horse.'

She smirked, and took several steps into the direction of Rose.

'And Lady Lilliane,' he called after her, as she rounded the corner, 'it would be best for all if you leave your tongue behind.'

Her aunt had not stopped looking at her since the stable boy had led Rose out all saddled up. Lilliane could almost read what she was thinking from the expression on her face. She supposed it wasn't proper for a lady to ride for such a long trip, yet her father had not protested to the plan. He did insist on them taking the carriage with them anyway; partly because Eliza was not a great horsewoman and partly because it was an easier way to transport her luggage. Perhaps he thought she would grow tired of riding too.

Sir Marsh had not objected to either. While her father was there he scarcely acknowledged her presence, barely speaking more than three words at a time. His continuing change in attitude infuriated her and she resolved once more to put this man, this stranger she had just met, out of her head.

As the moment of departure was almost upon them, Lily stood next to her horse, unsure of what to do next. Should she hug and kiss her father and aunt? Neither showed any sign of sadness over her departure. Her aunt was talking to Donovan, her father engaged in conversation with Lt Marsh. Sir Marsh clasped her father's hand one more time before moving over to his horse and mounting it. He glanced briefly at Lily, and then moved his gaze over their small crowd.

'Let's go men, say your last goodbyes.'

Mr Johansson and Lt. Marsh instantly rounded off their conversations and mounded their horses as well. Eliza was already seated in the carriage and Donovan climbed on it, next to John, ready to drive the horses the first couple of miles.

Lily decided she'd better not keep everyone waiting. Hesitantly she stepped away from Rose.

'Goodbye Mother, Father.'

'Goodbye Dear, I wish you a pleasant journey,' replied her father, patting her arm with his hand.

'Thank you Father.'

Her aunt kissed her cheeks fleetingly. 'Yes, goodbye, I hope we can expect you to behave on this trip... And at your destination,' she added, with a rise of her eyebrows.

Her father gave a bellied laugh. 'Come now Louisa, you and Lilliane raised her well. She is a good girl... a fine lady.'

Lily genuinely smiled. Her father had never given her such compliments. 'Thank you Father,' she said again, hugging him and kissing him on the cheek. At that moment she even felt sad about leaving him.

But not her... 'Child, hurry up. They are waiting for you,' her aunt said, disapproval evident in her voice.

Lily released her father, walked to Rose and mounted her. Within a minute Sir Marsh had given them another signal and they were off. Lily made sure to keep in the middle, away from Sir Marsh and close to Donovan and the carriage. As they crossed the first hill she looked back one last time at the castle, preparing to wave at her parents, but they had already gone inside.

3
Travels

It was past noon when Sir Marsh gave a signal to the group to stop for a break. The men slid off their horses and tied them to a nearby tree. Donovan halted the carriage, helping Eliza out.

Lily realised Sir Marsh had not been demeaning when he had recommended the carriage to her. The men rode at a steady pace and rarely paused. The carriage had no trouble keeping up; its horses and John the mender were used to travel. For her and Rose it was a different story. There was not one muscle in her body that didn't ache by the time they were halfway and she was pretty sure Rose was tired too. The mare had fallen behind a bit more with every mile passed.

Lilliane was tempted to pay a servant in the village to bring Rose back to the castle and ride in the carriage for the rest of the trip. They were still on her father's land after all. It would take at least another three days before they crossed into another region. A look at Sir Marsh made her reconsider though. She couldn't be sure, but thought that he was smirking at her; she resolved to not let him get the better of her. The thought that she was making a lot of resolutions when it came to this man was not fully acknowledged.

The men sat together and ate a meal of bread, meat and wine. Lily drank very little of the wine. She had never acquired a real taste for it. She preferred the water from their well, but while travelling all the available water went to the horses.

After their meal the men sat together and talked about the land they would soon travel through. It held no appeal to Lily; she could not add to the conversation. She knew very little of the surrounding land, and even if she had known something these experienced travellers did not, she was a woman; they would not consider her opinion as worthy to be heard.

Wandering away from the men, she sat in the grass and looked at the country around her. It was beautiful. Spring was at its highlight. The sun was shining, but a nice wind kept the temperature from rising too high. If it hadn't been for their destination and her company, Lily might even have enjoyed this trip.

She sat in the grass until it was time to resume their journey. The break had seemed too short, but she did not complain. She was determined to show them she was as tough as they were. As she prepared herself for several more hours of riding, she could feel someone standing close behind her. At first she thought it was her brother, but then the shadow the man cast over Rose was too long to be Donovan. Lilliane pretended not to notice. She stroked Rose and tightened the reins of her holster.

'I think you should ride in the carriage a bit.'

His voice was soft, yet she could hear it clearly. She sensed he was standing very close to her, even though she had not turned to see if she was right. The heat radiating from his body almost felt like the first rays of the sun did in the beginning of a morning.

Straightening her shoulders, she continued her work. 'I can assure you Sir; I am fine riding on Rose.'

'It is for Rose. She needs some time to get used to our pace and I think if I tie her reins to my saddle, she can adjust to travelling easier.' He grabbed a canvas bag from the ground and tied it next to where she was still adjusting straps, his hand slightly moving over hers as he tied the bag.

'Better for Rose? I guess if I can help her out that way, then travelling in the carriage would not be too awful.' She stroked the horse's mane.

'An excellent choice Milady. May I escort you to the carriage?'

Sir Marsh held out his arm. Lily nodded her head and laid her hand on his arm. They walked to the carriage and he helped her in. Lilliane sat down next to Eliza, clasping her hands together on her lap. Sir Marsh shut the carriage door and walked away. Halfway back to his horse, he glanced back to her and smiled. Lily smiled back, but could not meet his gaze. She was frightened by the amount of turmoil his touch had caused her insides.

Sir Marsh mounted his horse after tying Rose to his saddle by her reins. He gave the men a signal and it wasn't long before the entire group was in motion again. In the carriage Lily was asleep within minutes, her head once more filled with dreams about the strange man she was travelling with.

The carriage came to a halt so suddenly that Lily woke by violently falling forward. Next to her Eliza seemed to have been woken in the same way. Lily crawled back on the bench and poked her head out the window; before she could ask what was going on Lieutenant Marsh was already opening the door.

'Are you okay?' he asked, concern evident in his voice.

'Yes, thank you,' Lily answered for them both. 'What happened?'

'The bridge is out; we're approaching dusk. We did not see it until we almost stepped on it. The river is not too deep. We can cross it.'

Lily looked at the sky, then at the river. 'Surely Sir Marsh is not thinking of crossing the river now. We can barely see.'

Lt. Marsh shrugged carelessly. It was obvious he did not care much about a woman's opinion. 'I can assure you Lady Lilliane that my brother knows what he's doing.'

Lily decided to end this conversation quickly. Lt. Marsh was much less sophisticated compared to his older brother. 'Yes, of course.'

With Eliza on her heels, she exited the carriage towards the rest of the men. They were standing a few yards away; all still on their horses except for Donovan. Lily resolutely joined them, gazing directly into Sir Marsh's face. 'Sir Marsh, may I enquire to our plans for the rest of the day?'

'She sure does sound fancy, doesn't she?' one of the soldiers said to his friend, loud enough for everyone to hear.

Lilliane had avoided the four soldiers that accompanied them as much as possible. They were vulgar, uneducated men. A look from Sir Marsh silenced the soldier and his companion. He then turned to Lily, gazing at her for a full minute, still without speaking.

'We make camp here for the night and cross the river at daybreak. It will be easier at first light. You never know if a shallow river has treacherous parts.'

'Very well Sir,' replied Lily. She was exceptionally pleased with this decision and let him know by way of a soft smile.

He did not return it; instead he shouted orders to his men and dismounted his horse. The men went to work immediately. They prepared the horses for the night, made a fire and set up a shelter where the two ladies and Donovan could sleep. It was unthinkable for the ladies to sleep near the other men. If the carriage had been bigger Eliza would have persuaded Lilliane to sleep in there, but the floor was not big enough even for one to sleep on.

Eliza complained about sleeping outside, but Lily paid her no attention. She was excited about sleeping outside, something her brothers had done often, but had been thought improper for a female.

Donovan hung canvas cloths on the sides of their shelter to shield them all from the outside world. Eliza prepared their beds for the night, while Lily sat with Rose and untangled her mane. The mare had made it through the second part of the voyage better than the first part.

At dinner Lily drank more of the wine than she had done at the earlier meal, yet she still did not like the taste of it as it slid down her throat. Her worst thirst lessened, she passed the bottle to Eliza and did not drink anymore. The food was better. Eliza had brought several of her mother's pastries with her and they had bought bread and meat at the last village they had passed. Lily ate as much as she could. The journey had not improved her appetite.

She broke away from the men, walking along the outer lines of their campsite. The journey would prove to be very interesting if this first day was any indication to go by. Stopping at the riverbank, Lily inhaled the smell of the water. She had always loved the water. Her mother had taken her to a small river near the castle every week when she was a child. She could still see herself running over the grounds, her mother close on her heels. Lady Lilliane had not cared about proper manners everywhere. She was not like her sister. Aunt Louisa was not a free sprit like her mother had been.

'I brought you something.'

Lilliane turned at sound of Sir Marsh's voice. She had been so deeply consumed by memories of her mother she had not heard him approach. In his hands he held a bottle filled with liquid. She recognised it as a bottle of wine.

'No thank you, I am not thirsty.'

He held out the bottle, ignoring her protest and she took it in her hands. The liquid did not smell as wine, she took a sip as to not offend him and found to her surprise it was water not wine at all. Lily looked at him in question.

'You can keep that with you. You need to keep your strength up by drinking enough. There is plenty of water around here for the horses.' Without saying anymore, he turned and walked away.

'Sir Marsh...' she heard herself say. She was still surprised by this gesture of goodwill.

He turned back to look at her.

'Thank you Sir Marsh.'

'You're welcome Milady.' Bowing his head slightly, he turned and walked away.

Lily went the other way, back to Eliza and her brother. She kept the bottle of water close by and soon fell asleep with a smile on her face.

4
Feelings

It was nowhere near their noon break time but it had been over an hour since Lily had had enough of riding. The first two hours she had ridden in the carriage, trying to calm Eliza down. The poor girl was almost at the end of her wits. Lily was mad at Sir Marsh for not being more considerate of the girl. She tried very hard not to take it out on Rose. It wasn't the mare's fault the man was an arrogant snob.

The day had started off fine. Donovan had awoken them and while Eliza helped Lily get dressed, the men prepared the morning meal. They ate in relative silence. Lily had nothing new to report and the soldiers were not interesting enough to listen to. She kept her distance from them as much as she could, figuring that Sir Marsh must have told them to do the same. They certainly did not seek her company.

Donovan took their makeshift shelter apart after breakfast. Everyone was preparing themselves to cross the river. Lily had noticed Eliza was acting peculiar. She tried to get her to open up, but the maid was amazingly tight-lipped for once. It was only when they were almost going to cross that she remembered something; Eliza could not swim. The river was not too deep for the horses to cross, but it had dangerous undercurrent. They could not sit in the carriage; added weight might make it sink or at the very least make it difficult for the horses to pull it to the other side. Their baggage was lifted across by a crude rope bridge, but they had to cross over on horseback themselves.

Lily could feel Eliza tense up next to her as they watched the men move their supplies to the other side. The carriage would be next; it would take the highest amount of concentration for the men to get it across. Lily rose and resolutely walked up to Sir Marsh. She looked at him intently, waiting until he acknowledged her presence. It took several minutes, but he finally looked at her.

'Can we talk privately Sir?' said Lily, gesturing to a patch of trees a few yards from where they were standing.

The soldier standing behind him gave a hearty laugh. Lily ignored him.

'Very well Milady.' Sir Marsh followed her slowly, though she had asked for him alone, Lt. Marsh followed them as well.

Lilliane squeezed her hands together; unsure of how to start now that she actually had his full attention. 'It's about Eliza and the crossing. She is not very good at swimming.'

Lt. Marsh raised his chin. 'I can assure you Madam, we are making sure everyone will be safe.'

'I only want to make the matter clear,' resumed Lily, slightly annoyed by the interruption.

If it had been Sir Marsh she might have found it less intruding, but the Lieutenant should hold his tongue in front of a high ranking officer. As much as a woman had to in front of a man.

She paused, inwardly counting to ten. 'All I mean to say is…. Actually, all I request is, if you could please watch her closely while crossing.'

Sir Marsh gave a brisk nod. 'Of course Madam, the Lieutenant will take care to stick by her.'

'Thank you Sir,' said Lily, curtsying. She knew he was sincere and was pleased that he seemed to understand.

As she followed them back to the others, she noticed John, Donovan and the soldiers working under Mr Johansson's orders to make the final preparations on the carriage before it was to cross. She stood next to Eliza as John guided the horses and the carriage into the water. Eliza looked terrified at the thought of having to go next, making Lilliane glad she had asked Sir Marsh for extra help.

The carriage made it safely to the other side in less time than they had thought it would need. Lily walked to Rose and mounted her. She waited until Sir Marsh signalled her to come forward, unsure of who was going with Eliza apart from Lt. Marsh, but when Sir Marsh told her to go into the water, she forgot all about Eliza for the moment and concentrated on guiding Rose safely across. She had to admit she felt safe with Sir Marsh next to her, she was aware that he was taking exceptional care of her.

They were almost halfway when a scream came from behind them, its undertone of pure hysteria sending chills up Lily's spine. She halted Rose and turned sideways to see what was going on, just in time to see Eliza being pulled away by the current of the water. Lieutenant Marsh and two soldiers had been waiting to cross with Eliza. When it was their turn to go they had completely forgotten about the girl and went in without her. Eliza, even more scared to be left alone than to go into the water, had gone after them. Her horse had already been unnerved by her behaviour and the young girl, an inexperienced rider, soon lost control and fell off the horse. The current was strong. She was trying very hard to keep herself above water. Lily stood frozen in fear.

Sir Marsh turned to her; 'Lady Lilliane, keep going, get yourself ashore.' He then turned his horse and quickly drove it towards Eliza through the water. Lily did as she was told, dismounting as soon as Rose had solid ground under her hooves again.

Lily watched in terror as Eliza seemed to drift away faster than Sir Marsh was going. The girl had been lucky enough to cling to some driftwood. Lily was sure she would have gone under otherwise. It seemed like forever till he had reached Eliza and pulled her onto his horse.

Donovan stood next to his sister and patted her arm. 'She is safe now Lily, it's over.'

Lily did not reply. It wouldn't be truly over until they were both out of the water. She continued to watch in agony. The horse seemed to move so slow through the water, with its precious load on its back. It was only when its front legs touched the bank of the river that she dared to breathe again.

Sir Marsh immediately dismounted, then helped Eliza off. Lily was by her side in an instant, wrapping the girl in a quilt. She wanted to make sure she was alright, but she also wanted to tell off Sir Marsh. Her aunt would say it was improper, yet the young girl always thought of her mother in these kinds of situations. Lady Lilliane would have said something, anything, just to make sure that it would not happen again. As far as she was concerned, Sir Marsh was to blame, He had been wrong in letting his brother help Eliza cross. He should have done it himself.

Sir Marsh dropped to his knees and panted for breath. He was as wet as Eliza was after dropping off his horse to pull her on it properly. John draped a blanket over him and gave him some wine to warm himself. Lily realised that her feelings had to wait for later; he was not in a state to hear them now.

Lilliane guided Eliza to the carriage. The girl was already somewhat calmer. Lily sat beside her until she had drifted off to sleep. As she exited the carriage, she was surprised to see the men preparing themselves to continue their travels. Surely everyone needed more time to calm after the frightening event they had all witnessed. It had barely been fifteen minutes. The men told her nothing more than that it was on Sir Marsh's orders. She looked around to see if she could spot him, but saw him nowhere. Frustrated with everything that had happened and especially with that man, Lily decided to take a walk along the riverbank to clear her mind. She kicked some pebbles away with her foot.

'Direct hit Lady Lilliane.' Sir Marsh sounded amused, even as he was dusting the pebbles and sand off his arms. He had been partially hidden by a large willow tree growing near the water. The last pebbles gone, he rose from where he had been tying his shoes.

Lily swallowed, hardly remembering what she had wanted to say to him. It was obvious he had secluded himself to change out of his wet clothes. Lily tried hard not to gawk at the second sighting of his naked chest in less than three days. She thought of how scared Eliza had been and attempted to focus on his face instead of his body.

Sir Marsh continued to dry himself, before taking a clean shirt in his hands. 'Is there something I can help you with Milady?'

The question seemed so absurd coming from a half-naked man that it helped clear Lily's mind. 'It seems we are leaving?'

Marsh pulled his shirt on. 'Yes, that is true. So far we have only crossed the river today.'

'I thought perhaps, in light of what happened just now, it would be good for us, if we were to take a break.'

'Lady Lilliane, we are travelling over three hundred miles. It's not very safe anywhere with the war going on and we have two women and two young boys in our midst. Incidents like these are bound to happen. It is best to keep going.'

Clenching her teeth, Lily took a moment to think of what to say. 'As you wish Sir. I shall be ready when you want to leave.' She turned without another word, disappointed in him.

She thought he had understood her earlier, but it sounded like he was blaming Eliza for what had happened. If the men had done what she had asked, it would not have happened.

'Lady Lilliane?'

She continued walking, ignoring his words. She only stopped when she felt his hand on her arm. She glanced at his hand, then at his face. It was highly improper to touch someone, if they were caught like this out in the open, her reputation would be in danger.

'How is the girl?'

'Eliza is shaken up, but she will be fine. Her brother is watching her until I return. She is probably still sleeping. I should get back before she wakes.' She glanced at his hand again and furrowed her brow. Sir Marsh did not seem to take the hint.

'Her brother?'

'John. He manages the carriage for us.'

'Oh yes, of course… I didn't realise… we should go.'

Releasing her arm, he walked back to the camp. Lily was still angry at him and made no attempt to keep up. As they joined the others, Sir Marsh went directly to his men, while Lily headed for the carriage. John told her his sister had woken up once from a nightmare, but seemed fine otherwise. Opening the door, Lilliane climbed into the carriage and sat down next to the sleeping Eliza. No matter how many times he asked her about Eliza or would touch her arm, she was still angry with him about it all.

Even if he did make her toes curl.

5
Injury

Lilliane could hardly believe it, yet the sight before her was not a mirage. After a day that had a horrible start and an afternoon filled with nothing but the clicking of hooves on gravel, they were actually stopping early for the night. And not only that, they were in fact spending the night at an inn. Though they had only spent one night sleeping outside, the two days travelling had both physically and mentally tired her out.

Lily was looking forward to a normal bed inside a room and maybe even a bath if the inn had those on hand. She could make Eliza bring her dinner to her room and could spend the entire evening away from Sir Marsh. Her feelings of anger had slowly melted away during the afternoon, but a part of her was still cross with him. Something about him was bothering her immensely and she was looking forward to an evening of solitude to try to figure it out.

She booked a room for herself, with a bed for Eliza as well. The room held a small bathroom with a bath and a smaller tub to wash hands or face. She had already told the innkeeper that she planned to take full advantage of their accommodations.

It was almost time for dinner to be served downstairs. Despite her earlier resolutions, Lily decided to eat with the others, sharing a table with Eliza, John and Donovan. It was only Mr Johansson and Lt. Marsh at the next table. The soldiers were taking care of the horses and no one had explained where Sir Marsh had gone off to. Lily told herself she did not care.

Dinner progressed nicely along. She felt happy being with her two companions and her brother. After dinner, she sent Eliza to check on Rose and to order hot water for her bath, while she went to her room by herself. Lily followed the footman up to room twenty and entered after he opened the door.

The room was larger than she had imagined for an inn in such a small village. It was very pleasing looking. Shutting the door behind her, Lilliane lowered herself on the bed and closed her eyes. She was looking forward to an evening of blissful seclusion.

'Are you in the habit of entering other people's rooms Lady Lilliane? Or is it just my room you can not seem to stay away from?'

Lily kept her eyes closed a moment longer. She was certain she was hearing things. How was it otherwise possible that she again found herself in a room with him alone?

'Are you sleeping Lady Lilliane?'

This caused her to open her eyes and sit up. She looked at him; he was standing in the doorway to the bathroom, his trademark smirk on his face. At least this time he was fully dressed. 'Sir, there must have been a mistake. Room twenty is my room for the night.'

'Room twenty?' The look on his face turned to surprise. 'Is this not room nineteen?'

Lily shook her head. It was her turn to be amused. 'No Sir, I am sure this is twenty.'

Sir Marsh started to gather his things. Lily had not even noticed them around the room. All she had seen was the bed. He looked very embarrassed, beyond what she had ever seen him. She tried her best not to laugh, but when he grimaced and touched his shoulder in pain all thoughts of laughter were behind her.

'Is something the matter Sir?' she asked, concerned

'No, I am alright.' He tried to mask the pain, but Lily could see his shoulder was bothering him somehow.

She rose from the bed and took the two steps towards him. 'What's wrong with your shoulder?'

He smiled, trying to avoid the question. 'Oh nothing, just an old war wound. It opened up a little after I scraped it over some rocks in the water earlier.'

'While you were saving Eliza, you mean?' asked Lily, 'Let me see.'

She made to lower his shirt at the shoulder.

Sir Marsh took a step backwards. 'No, no Milady. A woman of your stature should not see it, it can not be seen with my shirt on.'

Lily grinned. 'Then take your shirt off Sir. It is nothing I have not seen before.'

She looked away and bit her lip. How bold she was being; she could hardly believe it herself sometimes. 'What I meant to say is, I've had some practise in nursing wounds. I might be of some use. I even have some medicines and bandages in my bag.'

Lily went to her bag and grabbed the pouch she always carried with her. Sir Marsh was still standing there, undecided on what to do. She chose for him by grabbing his arm and guiding him to the bed, making him sit down.

'Well, come on then,' she told him, still unable to keep the smirk off her face. 'I can't very well help you with your wound with your shirt on. I promise I won't tell anyone about what I have seen.'

Sir Marsh could not help but grin in return. 'No, I suppose you wouldn't, because it wouldn't look very good on you either.' Despite his mischievous reply, he still did what she had told him to do and removed his shirt.

The wound had been crudely bandaged. She guessed he had done it himself, too proud to ask anyone else for help. Removing it, she could not help but gasp a little when she saw how deep the cut had been. It had healed well over time, but it was still very tender. Bruises circled around it. She could tell these were fresh, even if the wound was not.

'A war wound?' she asked him, moving her fingers softly over it.

He sucked in a breath. 'Yes, I was practising sword-techniques with my brother and he struck me in a moment that I was not paying attention. It was not on purpose. Our mother was very angry at him, but it was not his fault. I was the one who had let my mind wander off.'

Lily shuddered at the story, even though she had not been there. It sounded like something she would have gotten upset about too and she could sympathise with Mrs. Marsh.

'I gather Lieutenant Marsh is very good with his sword,' she said, grabbing a special ointment from her bag and mixing it with some herbs.

'It was not with John, it was with my elder brother Edmund. He died in the war last year... As did my father.' Sir Marsh said this slowly, his eyes downcast at the floor. 'I inherited the title from my father after Edmund's death, but I would gladly give it up if it meant getting my brother back. John.... John and I... John is a good brother, but Edmund and I were much closer... I'm sure my mother misses my father as well.'

Lily had finished mixing the cream with the herbs, but she did not proceed with the next step of applying it. She could see that Sir Marsh was deep in thought and did not want to disturb him, even though his memories were painful. She thought of her own mother, gone for so long. She still missed her every day and realised it must be difficult for him too, since it had only been a year.

He looked up and smiled, the moment of thoughtfulness passed. 'What is that Lady Lilliane?' he asked curiously, pointing to the balm in her hands.

'It's a mixture. My mother wanted to teach me, she was very good with herbs. After she passed away, my nurse Beth taught me all my mother had educated her on. It will reduce the pain and make the swelling less.' She started to smear the cream on his bruised shoulder. 'All this from a brush with some rocks?'

'Yes,' he paused, 'To be honest, I also bumped into the door earlier.' he added, laughing.

She had to laugh too. It was not often a man of his standing would admit to being clumsy.

'I have my fair share of cuts and bruises from bumping into things. They say I usually have my head up in the clouds.'

'You, Lady Lilliane? No, that's not possible.' He smirked at her again. Blushing at his answer, Lily decided not to respond to him this time.

She worked in silence for several minutes, a comfortable one that enveloped them like a warm blanket on a cold summer night. After applying the ointment, she added a piece of fabric, cut from a clean cloth and bandaged it the way her mother and Beth had taught her. Surely, no blood would seep from it this way. Sir Marsh did not flinch at all, though when she looked at the cut, she knew it must hurt every time her fingers touched it. His eyes never wavered from her face.

Lily focused entirely on the wound and job at hand. She was definitely not mad at him anymore from that morning's accident. Instead she had gone back to feeling overwhelmed by the sheer presence of him close by. Thoughts of their objective and why she was travelling away from her home were kept firmly in her mind, yet again she was determined to put this man out of her mind. She had to believe that if her father had not been opposed to the match, he would have said so and would not have sent her away.

After finishing with dressing the wound, Lilliane organized her leftover materials and cleaned them up.

'You can put your shirt back on,' she said, still not looking at his face, fully aware that he had not stopped staring at her since they stopped talking. 'I will check the hallway to see if the coast is clear for you to go to your own room. I think our luck is just about to run out. Eliza should be back soon. She only had to check on Rose and order warm water for me.'

'Yes, I think that's a good idea,' replied Sir Marsh, as he pulled his shirt slowly over his head without trying to move his shoulder.

Lily hesitated, but then decided to help him pull the shirt on. Their task done, she planned to move away towards the door when he grabbed her hand in his. She slowly looked at him, and then stared at her hand. Before she could ask what he was doing, he lifted her hand to his mouth and kissed her fingers... One soft kiss.

'Thank you for your help Lady Lilliane,' he whispered, releasing her hand.

She swallowed. 'You're welcome Sir Marsh.' Lily quickly moved towards the door and opened it far enough to poke her head out. 'There is no one here,' she said to him, opening the door all the way.

Sir Marsh grabbed his bag, walking passed her. He looked to both sides to see which way room nineteen was. After finding out it was the left one, he quickly opened the door.

Lilliane was still standing in the doorway of her own room, looking at him. He hesitated, holding the door handle in one hand. 'Good night Milady.'

She nodded. 'Good night Sir.' They both proceeded to close the door.

Lily leaned against the door on the inside, trying to get control back over her heart. What if the walls in this inn were so thin he could hear it beating? She could still feel where his lips had touched her fingers.

The door started to move from the outside. Lily moved away and lowered herself on the bed. She realised she was sitting where he had been seated moments ago and quickly moved to the left.

Eliza came in, carrying a large pail full of water. 'I have your warm bathwater here, Lady Lilliane. I will prepare the bath for you now.'

'Ah yes.' Lily breathed in deeply in an effort to control herself, but Eliza did not seem to notice anything was amiss.

Eliza went into the bathroom with the pail. Lily stayed on the bed, leaning back. She closed her eyes. She had desired a night alone without Sir Marsh, but already knew this evening would be spent with him not far from her mind.

6

Wandering

Lily opened her eyes and was surprised to see total darkness around her. It took her a full minute to realise it was still the middle of the night and everyone was sleeping. Something in the night had been disturbing enough to awake her from her slumber. She did not often wake up during the night, but when she did, she always had trouble falling back to sleep.

Finding nothing out of the ordinary other than the sounds of night in the inn, she rolled over to her other side and closed her eyes again. It was no use though, sleep would not come back.

Across the room, Eliza was still sleeping peacefully. Lily had no intention of waking the girl. It had been a difficult and tiring day and she was almost sure that the coming day would be very tiring too. Throwing the covers off, she climbed out of bed and casually made her way over to the window. Lilliane sat down on the windowsill, drawing the curtains back far enough so she could gaze outside. The little village looked lovely in the moonlight. It was a full moon and there were many stars shining brightly. The darkness of the night was only interrupted by the shining of the moon and the shadows it cast on the sleeping village.

Lily continued to look outside, clearly delighted with what she saw. It was a spectacular view; behind the building she could see the mountains and the river they had crossed earlier. Across the road were the stables that belonged to the inn. It looked as quiet as the rest of the square. Or did it? Someone was making their way over the square and towards the other side of the road.

Blinking her eyes several times, she still did not let herself believe what she was seeing. Was there really someone creeping towards the stables? Had she seen correctly or were her eyes playing a trick on her, the night sky and her own drowsiness contributing to that. She looked again and saw the same person opening the stable doors. He was too tall to be a woman and in his manner of walking she could clearly distinguish a male, though she did not know who it was.

Lilliane leaned back against the side of the windowsill. She decided to wait until he came out again. She yawned as time slowly passed by. Maybe there had been no one? Perhaps it really had been a figment of her imagination. Just when she was about to give up, the stable doors opened again and the same black form came out. Lily watched with wide eyes as the black form made his way back to the inn. She thought she distinguished a uniform in the moonlight, but could not be sure about the colour, rank or anything else. The inn's door closed with a loud bang, telling her the figure had gone back inside. Turning the curtains back to their original place, Lily walked back to her bed and got in. She felt cold in the night air and snuggled deeply under the covers, thinking about what she had seen. Who would get out of bed in the middle of the night just to go into the stables? What had he done in the stables? Had the opening of the inn's door been the thing to wake her earlier? She could not be sure. She could not be sure of anything. It had been an oddity she would not soon forget. The drowsiness started to take control of her again; she closed her eyes. Unusual or not, the incident was not enough to keep her awake and she fell back into a dreamless sleep.

The next morning a cheerful Eliza woke her as she always did. Breakfast was served in bed by her maid, after being brought up by a manservant. When she was finished, and had dressed as well, she went downstairs to see if the others were up. Eliza went down to the servants' kitchen to eat her own breakfast. She could see nothing of Sir Marsh, her brother, Lt. Marsh or any of the soldiers in the dinning-room or den of the inn. Still seeing no one else after five minutes of waiting, Lily resolved to visit Rose, just so she could have someone to talk to.

She left the inn and walked towards the stable, the memory of the night came back to her fully as she realised that whoever she had seen go into the stables had walked the same path she was taking now. It was a curious thing to do in the middle of the night but the inn was very crowded and there were several men who could fit the description of a person covered in blackness sneaking in the middle of the night. She opened the stables door, surprised to hear voices and recognised them instantly. The soldiers were standing near the horses, talking loudly in the obnoxious way that she usually ignored. She realised as she came closer that they were actually talking about Eliza and the incident with the river the previous morning.

'As if it's my fault the silly servant girl almost drowned. Sir Marsh was so angry about it he took all my privileges away for two complete weeks.'

The other guards grunted. 'Yeah, we know, we have the same punishment. Only young Robert was not punished. Even the Lieutenant had to bear the brunt of Sir Marsh's anger.'

'Well I say, it was well deserved,' said a younger sounding voice.

Lily knew it was the Robert they mentioned earlier. The fourth soldier, and the youngest of them all was not as rude as the other three and mostly kept his tongue in front of her.

'Oy. Be quiet Robert,' replied the first one. 'That so called lady we are travelling with better not give us anymore trouble.'

A loud cough broke the man's rant. Lieutenant Marsh stepped forward and out of the darkness. 'Men,' he said loudly, 'are you almost done with those horses?'

'Yes Sir.' It sounded immediately from two of the men. The loudest did not reply, but made no other comment either. Even with his big mouth, he was quiet when in the presence of his superior.

Lily decided enough was enough and stepped out of the darkness herself. 'Good morning gentleman,' she said calmly, curtsying to Lt. Marsh and ignoring all but the youngest of the soldiers.

'Good morning Milady,' Lieutenant Marsh replied. He sounded brisker than she was used to. She assumed he was surprised to see her in the stables.

Rose was standing a couple of meters away from them. Lily walked past the men and stopped next to Rose, stroking the mare over her back as she often did in the morning.

The young soldier stopped beside her. 'Shall I prepare your horse for our journey Milady?' he asked shyly.

Lily nodded; she felt she had had enough of the stables and these men. 'That would be much appreciated,' she answered him in reply and left the stables again. She did not need to look back to know that Lieutenant Marsh was scolding the soldiers for their earlier words, even though he could not be sure she had heard them.

It took a few minutes before Lilliane went back inside the inn. The soldiers had enraged her with their talk about Sir Marsh and Eliza more than she would have ever imagined. She knew she could not expect anything else from uneducated men like them, but it still made her quite cross. Angry enough to tell Sir Marsh? She was not sure. They still had a very long way to go and she realised that these men could make it very difficult for them all. He had already punished them for leaving Eliza at the riverbank. Perhaps it was best to let the matter lie for now and let Sir Marsh deal with his own men.

She made her way into the den and saw Sir Marsh and Donovan were downstairs by now, accompanied by both John and Eliza.

Sir Marsh spotted her immediately and he quickly rose from the table. 'Good morning Milady,' he said with an obvious glance at her face. A soft smile grazed his features as he looked at her.

She blushed, but managed to compose herself quickly. 'Good morning Sir, good morning Donovan, John.' Lily sat down next to her brother.

'We were wondering about you,' Sir Marsh said, immediately engaging her in conversation.

'I was out for a morning walk and checking on Rose in the stable.'

'Are the men hard at work with the horses?'

'Yes Sir, I saw them there. They are preparing them for our journey as we speak.'

Lily looked at Donovan and the others, trying to encourage them to participate in the conversation. Seeing Sir Marsh so suddenly in the den unnerved her a bit. She could still feel the ghost of his lips on her fingers, as well as the warmth of his body close by.

Knowing that she couldn't talk to Sir Marsh very long without blushing intently, Lily turned to her brother and engaged him in conversation instead, the others listening, occasionally adding their two cents. Interruption came in the form of Mr Johansson and Lt. Marsh, who came to tell them the horses were ready.

Sir Marsh stood from the table and held out his arm to Lily. 'Are you ready Milady?'

The Last Lord's Wife

Lily nodded, not trusting her own voice as she placed her hand over his. The feeling of his hand touching her felt comfortable and familiar. She blushed even more as he guided her outside, relieved that everyone else was walking behind them.

Part of her felt thankful when he released her hand. The horses and carriage were already outside the stables. Robert the soldier was standing next to Rose, holding her reins in his hands. Lily smiled and thanked him for his assistance. She mounted Rose and waited until Sir Marsh told them they were going. Eliza had already climbed into the carriage and everyone seemed ready except for Sir Marsh himself. He had not mounted his horse yet, instead he was fidgeting with his saddle and the reins. The others waited patiently, unsure of what their leader was doing, yet knowing it was best to stay silent. Finally, he mounted and guided his horse a few hesitating steps forward. When it seemed everything was fine, he guided him a little faster. Lily watched him curiously. Something inside her told her something was wrong. Perhaps the horse was feeling ill or it was Sir Marsh himself who was not feeling well. She did not know. Before she could ask if something was wrong, she suddenly did not see Sir Marsh on his horse anymore. He had fallen off; saddle and all.

Very quickly, Lily dismounted, followed by Lieutenant Marsh and Donovan. The others dismounted, but held their ground. Lily kneeled next to the fallen man, while Lieutenant Marsh led the horse a few steps away. Donovan kneeled next to his sister.

'Are you injured Sir?' she asked, frightened.

His eyes were open wide. He was conscious, which relieved Lily, but seemed to be a bit dazed. Instead of answering Lilliane, he held out his hand to Donovan. 'Help me up, will you lad.'

43

Lily placed her hands on his shoulders and pushed him down. 'I really must protest Sir, you may have broken something.'

Sir Marsh looked to be annoyed at her. 'I can assure you madam, I am fine.' He gazed into her eyes and saw the fear that was obvious. His expression changed to something Lily did not fully understand. 'Really I am...' he repeated in a softer voice for only her to hear.

A trickle of blood seeped from a cut on his forehead. He casually wiped it away and gestured for Donovan to help him up. Lily rose too and followed him to his horse.

'At least let me put a bandage on that cut Sir.' She tried again.

'Dear lady, it is not necessary. All that is needed is some water to wash the wound out and some wine to help my brother back on his horse.' Lieutenant Marsh tittered at his own joke. Lily made no reply. 'I do not know what you do with your equipment brother; your saddle's strap has torn right down the middle,' continued Lt. Marsh, laughing again.

Sir Marsh gave a bemused headshake. His horse was ready for him again. Sir Marsh mounted it under the watchful eye of Lily. She wanted to shout at him for being so pigheaded, but was glad to see him secure in the saddle once more. Turning back, she remounted Rose and was ready to go as soon as he gave the sign to continue their journey. Before long Lily was deep in thought, trying to discover for herself why she seemed to care so much about this infuriating man.

7
Confusion

Rose was tired; Lily could tell that by the way the mare could hardly keep up with the others. She was tempted to ask for a break, but resolved against it. Hardly a word had been spoken between her and Sir Marsh. Lily wanted to keep it that way.

This man, he could infuriate her so. One moment he was setting her skin aflame, the next, he worked up her temper. She supposed she should have expected it. After all, he was a man and a noble one to boot. She had rarely met a nobleman who was not full of himself in some way or another…

And yet…

Her thoughts were interrupted by a group of six men galloping towards them on an intersecting course. They were clad in uniform and one carried the flag of their noble King's army. Sir Marsh held up his hand to halt the group. The unknown men rode up close enough to talk to them. Lily noticed they were heavily armed with rifles. She shivered. The soldiers kept their weapons within reach, ready to be used if any of them were to try something. She knew this was a dangerous time with the war going on, but still felt unnerved by it. Sir Marsh gestured for her to move behind him, but she stayed where she was. Her stubbornness earned her a annoyed look.

'Halt, in the name of our King.'

Sir Marsh did not point out they had already stopped, 'Good day to you Sir, I am Sir William Roderick Marsh of Castle Locksgate. Who do I have the pleasure of addressing?'

'Sir, I am Captain Thomas Crawford, proud to be a part of the King's army. These are my men. We travel these roads to keep them safe for the King's good people. We must ask you for your travel-papers and destination Sir.'

Sir Marsh nodded towards his brother who immediately retrieved a large pack of bound papers from his bag. 'We are travelling to our great capital, to deliver this lady, Lady Lilliane Gaeli of Geastwood Castle, to the convent there. Travelling with us are her brother Donovan Gaeli, her lady's maid Eliza, our horse-mender John, my brother Lieutenant John Lennard Marsh, Mr James Johansson and these four soldiers are Lucas Fletcher, Henry Fletcher, Marcus Peterson and Robert Pike.' Sir Marsh pointed at them all as he called out their names.

Captain Crawford looked through their papers with interest. 'Not many that we have met are going to the capital. Is she bound for…' he fell quiet.

'Yes,' replied Sir Marsh abruptly. 'She is. I trust you find our papers in order?' he continued, ignoring the curious look on Lily's face.

'Yes Sir, have a pleasant journey.' Captain Crawford handed the papers back to Lieutenant Marsh and clicked his heels in greeting. He eyed Lily for a moment longer, but said nothing, then rejoined his men. Sir Marsh nodded to his brother, who gave the order to go. Lily rode next to Sir Marsh. She kept shooting curious looks towards him, but when she realised he was avoiding her eyes on purpose, she gave up and concentrated on the road again. She was sure she would find out sooner or later.

Lily pulled her wrap tighter around her shoulders. She felt chilly in the evening-air. Everybody was fast asleep; she was the only one from their group who was awake. Eliza, John and Donovan were sleeping in a new shelter the boys had set up. The others were sleeping around the fire.

Marcus Peterson was supposed to be on watch, but he had fallen asleep. Lily decided against waking him. She could not stand his company for longer than a few minutes. He and his two companions could not have a sensible conversation with anyone but themselves. She could keep watch if it was needed.

A few feet away from their camp, a big rock stood next to the road, Lily had climbed up on it and sat down. Her feet were dangling over the edge and her back was towards the others. The moon was as bright as the night before, but this evening there were no buildings in their vicinity. Lily had had trouble sleeping since putting her head down on the pillow. Sir Marsh was present in her mind all day; he had been since she had seen him fall from his horse earlier. She knew he had said he was fine, but could not help but look at him from time to time. She caught every frown and grimace, accumulating all to his shoulder or the cut on his face. Had he been brave in his denial of pain? Lily rubbed her hands together and frowned. Men. Why did they insist in being so proud all the time.

A noise from behind her made her look over her shoulder. Was someone from their group waking up? It seemed to be so; one of the men had stood up from his sleeping place and was now rummaging. Lilliane could not see who it was. She squinted her eyes, but a cloud shading the moonlight made it impossible to distinguish one man from another. She only knew it wasn't Sir Marsh, she would have instantly known if it had been him. Whoever it was had finished what he intended to do and went back to his sleeping place. Lily had no idea if the sleepwalker had done anything she should be alarmed about. She didn't trust the soldiers and even Lieutenant Marsh was not on her list of trustworthy men. She couldn't be sure about Mr Johansson, they had not conversed enough for her to form an opinion about him.

Truth be told, the only ones she really felt comfortable with were her brother and the two servants. Lily smiled at her own thoughts and added Sir Marsh to that little list as well. True, he could be conceited, but in the next moment he was suddenly so nice. Was he as sweet as he seemed sometimes or was it all an act? The only thing she did know was that he was a complete mystery to her; unfortunately, that notion did not help her one bit.

Lily sighed, rising from where she had been sitting. It was no use sitting here and wasting the night away thinking, she may as well lie in bed and do the very same thing. At least she would be warmer there. She turned and carefully climbed off the rock.

A noise from beside her made her glance at the campfire group again. Perhaps the mysterious wanderer from before had woken again. Lily stopped, for a moment too surprised to continue walking, she mentally scolded herself and put on a neutral expression. Lt. Marsh was standing, leaning against a tree. How long he had been there she didn't know, but it did not look as if he had just arrived there. Smoke blew from his mouth and nose, the movement of his hand holding the pipe was the only motion she could distinguish. He did not even blink his eyes, only continued to stare at her.

Lilliane managed a weak smile and a nod as she passed. It seemed to break the spell he was under as he nodded back and even grinned. Yet Lily was still unnerved and was glad to climb into bed next to Eliza again, happy her brother was nearby.

8
Ambush

Lily was awoken by a sound that instantly chilled her to the bone. The sound of metal hitting metal echoed through their camp. Eliza had left her bed and the lifted curtain that normally separated the two boys from the girls, showed her they were absent too. Where was everybody? What was going on and why had they not woken her? Again, metal hit metal. Lily rose quickly, pulled her wrap around her in one perfected motion, and left her shelter. She did not know what she expected to see, but certainly not what was happening.

'Donovan, John, is that really necessary?' she scolded them, she couldn't help it. The sound of fighting, whether mock or for real, had never appealed to her. It scared her too much.

The young men stopped when they heard her. Donovan looked ruffled.

'It's fine Lilliane. We have done this before, besides...' he turned sideways and pointed at something. 'They are enjoying it.'

Lily followed to where he gestured and was surprised to see their entire group of men and Eliza, sitting together. It was obvious that they had been enjoying themselves before she appeared. Only Sir Marsh was separated from them all. He was doing something with a book and quill.

Lily knew nothing she could say would change anything. She huffed and turned back to the shelter. 'Eliza,' she shouted, even as she walked away. The maid quickly scrambled to her

49

feet and followed her mistress. Eliza knew her lady was angry and that this would not be a pleasant encounter.

Breakfast was served less than an hour later. Lilliane sat between Donovan and Sir Marsh. She conversed very little with either, not in the mood for the typically forced small talk. Eliza, sitting next to her brother a few feet away, was quiet too. Lily supposed she might have been too hard on the girl earlier. It was true she had her father's temper. There was nothing to do about it now though. She could not make amends with the girl while everyone was watching and truth be told she had two other things that were far more pressing on her mind.

Sir Marsh was sitting so close, they almost rubbed elbows if one of them moved. Lilliane tried to stay as still as possible, Sir Marsh however was doing no such thing. Every time they nearly touched, Lily's heart skipped a beat. Something else, less pleasant, was taking a lot of the present thrill away though. Across from her Lieutenant Marsh had hardly stopped looking at her. She knew Sir Marsh had noticed too from the expression he periodically sent to his brother. Where Sir Marsh's looks always made her blush and tingle, his brother's only unnerved her. She wished he would stop and did not return any of his glances.

When breakfast was over, Lily rose almost at the same time as Lt. Marsh did. Out of the corner of her eye, she saw him move towards her and quickly asked Sir Marsh to escort her to her horse, as she needed to ask him something.

'Very well Madam,' he said in reply and told the Lieutenant to prepare for their journey. Lt. Marsh looked like he wanted to protest, but wisely said nothing.

Lily and Sir Marsh slowly walked to Rose. Now that she had succeeded in getting away from Lt. Marsh, she had to think of something to actually ask him. Sir Marsh seemed to notice her helplessness. He smiled at her reassuringly. Whatever was going on between them, she realised it must be mutual. They were even developing a feel for each other's moods and habits. As they stopped next to her mare, they still had not talked since leaving the others.

Sir Marsh stroked Rose over her back.

'She's a fine looking horse.'

Lilliane kissed her mare on her nose and started to stroke her as well. 'Yes, she is indeed.'

'Did you have something to ask me Milady?' Sir Marsh grinned at her with that twinkle in his eyes.

Lily bit her lip softly and looked away for a moment, thinking of something to say. 'How's your shoulder?' she asked, still at a loss for something else to say.

'It's much better, thank you. That ointment of yours has worked miracles.'

'Glad to hear that. I should change the dressing soon.'

Sir Marsh smirked wider. 'Later perhaps, not everyone needs to see me half naked after all.'

Lily blushed deeply. She couldn't help but look away again. Sir Marsh took her hand in his. They were partially sheltered by Rose, but were still in plain sight of most of the others. Lily glanced to their hands in alarm, but sighed in relief when all he did was bow and kiss it rapidly. He had stepped back so quickly, she almost had to wonder if he had really kissed her hand again.

'I should tell the men to get ready.' Sir Marsh clicked his heels together and walked away from her. She tried not to watch him too conspicuously as he left and deeply wished they could be alone again, at the same time wondering if that was such a good idea.

Lily hastened Rose to follow Sir Marsh's horse. For some reason she had stuck by him ever since she started riding today. Usually she kept away from him more, conscious of getting unwanted attention focused on them and unsure of whether or not he would appreciate it. Today, however, she felt on edge about something. She supposed it to be because of the earlier incident with Lieutenant John Marsh, but something told her it was more than that.

Sir Marsh stopped his horse suddenly and gave the order for the others to do the same. None dismounted; they all waited for his next order. 'Stay on your horses men.' Sir Marsh shouted to them, dismounting himself. He took a few steps forward, seemingly looking for something, before going back to his horse and remounting it.

Lily looked on in confusion. She had absolutely no idea what was going on. Sir Marsh was acting very strange. Turning his horse Sir Marsh guided his stallion next to Rose. Lily grew more curious by the minute, especially when Sir Marsh leaned towards her and beckoned her to do the same.

'Yes Sir?' she whispered, not knowing why she did that.

'Perhaps it's best that you go and sit in the carriage with Eliza, Milady.'

Lily was quiet. 'Why Sir?' she finally managed to stagger out. She watched his expression change to something else that was even more unreadable.

'You might think I am mad.' He said it so softly even she had trouble hearing it.

She longed to reach out and touch him to reassure him somehow, but could not with everyone watching them so closely. 'Try me, Sir.'

'I have a feeling... Something is about to happen, I am just not sure what.' He almost laughed at himself, thinking that he sounded ridiculous; Lilliane was however not amused at all. She had had a feeling of dread of her own all day.

'Okay Sir, I will.' Her expression told him she was deeply serious. He mirrored her look, an undertone of gratitude mixed with it.

She started to guide Rose towards the carriage. Everyone else was still watching them; they had not heard the conversation and curiosity hung in the air. Lily was almost at the carriage. She would dismount Rose, give the mare's reins to Donovan and join Eliza in the carriage as it was the wisest thing to do right now.

Before her feet hit the ground, a loud bang was heard nearby. It seemed to be coming from all around them. A cloud of smoke filled the surrounding area, dissolving their line of vision immediately. Lily coughed, trying desperately to hold onto Rose with her other hand. The horses whinnied and several stomped their feet. Around her she could hear the men trying to calm them down, coughing themselves.

It took a few moments before the chaos had dissolved and the smoke ebbed away. Lilliane had not said a word; she was rapidly becoming very scared. During the commotion, she had heard footsteps, followed by a hand curling around her neck and something cold pressed equally hard. Someone was holding her hostage, she had no idea who it could be, or what his intentions were.

It was not until all the smoke had cleared that she could clearly see in what kind of dangerous situation they suddenly found themselves in. They were surrounded.

There wasn't anyone who did not have something pointed at them. One man had climbed into the carriage and held

Eliza at gunpoint, another sat next to John with a rifle. The man holding Lily stank of tobacco and gunpowder and kept breathing heavily near her ear. The cold thing she felt against her neck, she realised must be a dagger of some sort. Even the soldiers, who had been quick to try to draw their swords, were helpless against the men surrounding them.

'Welcome, monsieur, madam.'

Lily slowly turned towards the voice, she had no choice, the man with the dagger forced her to turn towards the man who was obviously their leader. He was not a tall man. Dressed in all black, his long black hair and beard accentuated his image. It was clear this was a dangerous man, a man used to getting whatever he wanted. Someone who would not hesitate to do them harm.

'What do you want?' Sir Marsh's voice never wavered.

'Just a friendly talk Sir.' The leader's smile was greasy, it disgusted Lily.

'A friendly talk?' Sir Marsh spat back. 'You are holding a gun on me. Your men are keeping my people prisoner.'

The man shrugged. 'An unfortunate necessity, I would hate to get the ending of any of your fine-made swords stuck in me.'

'Fine then, tell me what you want and we can resolve this, perhaps even without bloodshed.'

'Oh nothing special; just all your money, your jewellery and some of the horses. If you are nice, perhaps we shall let you keep your women.'

Donovan snarled, 'Watch your tongue. You are talking about Lady Lilliane Gaeli of Geastwood Castle.'

'Lady Lilliane…..?' The bandit laughed, making his men echo him. 'That, my lad, might mean something when you're home, but here it's every man for himself.' The men laughed tauntingly at their leader's joke.

'You are still on my father's land.' Donovan continued, working up a temper.

'Like I said, it means nothing here. Get him off his horse.... I fear you are not taking me seriously; perhaps the lad needs to be an example.' He gave a nod towards one of his men.

The man who had been holding the gun on Donovan, took the boy by his collar and dragged him off his horse. Donovan fell to the ground, his horse stomping his hooves dangerously close next to him. The man dragged him away and forced him onto his knees.

'What shall I do to him Sir?' the man asked with a grin. Lily shivered in angst.

'Do your specialty Milroy.' The others laughed again, a cruel cutting sound in Lily's ears. The man called Milroy took out a dagger.

'No, please!' Lily begged.

The leader pointed his finger at her. 'Hold her. Make sure she sees.'

The arm tightened around her neck and the knife pressed deeper as well. A trickle of blood seeped from the wound, but Lilliane did not feel it. She could only see Donovan being pushed to the ground by Milroy. The hand with the dagger went up. The next instant she closed her eyes, but that could not shut out her brother's blood chilling cry. She opened her eyes, cursing herself for her moment of cowardice. The dagger had pierced Donovan's left foot. The boy was still whimpering softly.

Donovan's cry had not been the only one piercing the air. Sir Marsh was furiously trying to dismount his horse even though there was still a rifle pointed at him. Only when his captive pressed the barrel of the gun against his belly did he stop his attempts. He could only show his discontent by loudly yelling. 'Alright. You've made your point. I am ordered to bring these two safely to the capital. I will give you our money and jewels if you give me your word and harm no one else.'

The leader grinned maliciously. 'We shall see… if you are hospitable, we shall take your terms, if you're not…' he let the rest linger in the air. The men snickered.

Lily could only shiver. She thought they were all as good as dead. Her brother had stopped whimpering softly. She could see he was fighting to stay awake. The boy had lost a lot of blood in a small amount of time.

Sir Marsh released a gush of air. 'No. If you do not give us your word that you will let all the men, and the two ladies, go unharmed I will not show you where I hid our money. I can assure you Sir, you will not find it without my help. Now, let us dismount and let me attend to the lad, he needs immediate assistance. Let the lady climb into the carriage next to the maid.'

Lily looked at him intensely, trying to see if Sir Marsh was taken seriously. The leader nodded and his men all took a step back, letting them all dismount.

Lily could feel the man with the dagger loosen his grip, yet he did not remove the knife. 'Before this is all over, you and I are going to have a little fun.' he whispered in her ear. She tried not to shiver at the tone of his voice, it repulsed her deeply.

Sir Marsh took control. 'Men, tie your horses to the trees then stand next to the carriage. Do nothing that will endanger us! John, help Donovan into the carriage. His sister can take care of the wound.' He glanced at Lily, still being held. 'Is letting Lady Lilliane go not a part of our agreement as well?' Sir Marsh steadied himself to his full length.

'Yes, I suppose you're right. Let her go Leopold.' The leader grinned, 'You may still have your fun later if the good Sir here does not obey.' The dagger was dropped. Lily did not waste time to add distance between herself and Leopold.

She almost ran towards the carriage. Sir Marsh was next to her in a heartbeat. 'Are you okay Milady?' he whispered.

'Yes Sir, are you?' Lilliane counteracted.

Sir Marsh nodded, 'What will happen now Sir?' she looked into his eyes, immensely afraid for them all.

'Don't worry Milady,' he replied, squeezing her hand, then quickly shut the door behind her.

Eliza took a handkerchief from her pocket and pressed it against Lily's neck. She had hardly registered it, far too busy watching Sir Marsh as he rejoined the others. She knew Donovan needed her help, but could not tear herself away from the window. Inside the carriage they could not hear what was said outside, but she could see the soldiers and Mr Johansson standing next to each other. Some of the bandits were still holding them at gunpoint, the others were following the conversation between Sir Marsh and their leader. Lieutenant Marsh was standing close to his brother.

The sounds of the carriage mixed together, an unheard blur of noise in the background of a sudden battle. Who had shot the first gun? Lily did not know, all she saw was Sir Marsh as he battled for his life, for all their lives. One of the capturers was down, caught unaware by a gunshot to the leg. Another soon followed as his dagger was struck from his hands. The men were no match for the well trained soldiers. Soon there were only a couple still standing. The leader battled feverishly with

Sir Marsh, matching his sword blow by blow. Lily watched with her hand in front of her mouth to muffle the screams.

The soldiers rounded up the fallen bandits, making sure none of them could do further harm by tying them up. Lieutenant Marsh kept a close eye on his fighting brother. Lily saw something move from the corner of her eye and unwillingly looked that way. Leopold, the man who had cut her, was still mobile. He was moving in the bushes next to the horses, aiming his rifle right at Sir Marsh. Did no one see him? Could the Lieutenant not see him? She thought she had seen a flicker of recognition in his eyes and he seemed to be looking the same way as she was.

There was no time to think it through; Lily threw the door open and jumped out. 'Sir Marsh, behind you!' her scream penetrated the air.

Leopold seemed to freeze, Sir Marsh immediately turned to her. The leader was the only one not paying attention to her; he bolted for the nearest horse and quickly rode off. Lieutenant Marsh aimed his weapon at Leopold; his finger hesitated on the trigger. Lily saw Leopold come from this daze and lift his own rifle. His finger was inches away from the trigger.

Lily screamed at John Marsh, 'Shoot!'

A gunshot echoed. The Lieutenant had not fired. Lily quickly looked at Sir Marsh, yet saw no obvious wounds. She then turned her gaze to Leopold only to see him drop his gun and sink to the ground. Mr Johansson lowered his rifle.

Sir Marsh breathed forcefully, looking at Lily. Anger was apparent on his face. 'Clean this mess up,' he shouted to the men, then stalked away.

Lily watched him leave, before going back into the carriage to take care of her brother.

9
Disagreement

Lady Lilliane Mariah Gaeli did not feel very ladylike preparing for the upcoming task. Donovan was sitting two feet away, already ready for it, but she was not moving in a steady pace herself. The poker was heating up in the fire. She needed to cauterise the wound to prevent infection. This part of her training had never been celebrated and now she had to do it with her brother….

She took the poker in her hand and turned around. Eliza had cleaned the wound and John found something for Donovan to bite down on. They were only waiting for her to continue.

Donovan bravely nodded at her, but Lily could do nothing but stand there. She wished for Sir Marsh to come and perhaps take over, knowing fully he had not sought her company since walking away earlier. Soft steps came up behind her. Lily's heart fluttered with hope, perhaps Sir Marsh was there to help her after all, but to her disappointment, it was Mr Johansson who took the poker from her. She gave it willingly; at least it meant not having to do it herself.

As Mr Johansson turned to do what she could not, Lily turned away from the group and wandered as far off as she dared. She could see Lieutenant Marsh talking to the man that had stopped them earlier, Captain Crawford. Some of the bandits were dead, the others would probably hang for their crimes. The Captain was taking them into custody, disposing of the dead as well. They had been lucky, none of their group was seriously injured, Donovan by far the worst.

Sir Marsh was standing in the water, immerged up to his waist. He was washing his shirt in the water, rinsing the blood out of it. Lily wanted to go to him and talk, but could see from the force in his movements that he was still angry about something. She leaned back against the tree, watching him as he submerged his body completely. Could she say anything that would lessen his anger? She was not even sure what he was angry about. Perhaps it was better to leave him alone. It wasn't like she couldn't use some time alone herself.

A loud scream broke the silence. Lily turned, but did not move further, knowing full well it was Donovan. She slid down the tree towards the ground. She did not care that it wasn't proper, that it was not something a lady would do. Emotionally she was too drained to keep herself up.

Sir Marsh got out of the water, stopping near her. He squeezed the water from his shirt then pulled it over his head. Lily knew he had seen her, but as long as he was not talking to her, she was not speaking to him either. He walked past her, still not acknowledging her. Lily tried not to be too upset.

'Lady Lilliane?'

Lily lifted her head, surprised. She had heard no one approach.

'Oh, I'm sorry, I didn't see you there.' Lieutenant Marsh smiled at her.

Lily felt uncomfortable. She did not quite believe his story of not seeing her; she thought she was rather hard to miss at this particular spot. 'That's alright,' she replied politely. 'Did Sir Marsh send you to fetch me?'

Lt. Marsh rubbed his forehead. 'William...? I mean, Sir Marsh... Oh no, I was just taking a walk by myself. Can I escort you back to the others?' The Lieutenant held his arm out. Lily hesitated; could she get away with refusing him or would that be too impolite. Before she could answer him, heavy footsteps were heard coming closer.

'Lieutenant. Did I not make my orders clear?' Sir Marsh stopped in front of his brother and looked at him crossly.

Lieutenant Marsh's stature changed within seconds. 'Yes Sir, I carried them out just like you told me to.'

'Then why did I find this among my possessions.' He held up a rifle. 'It is neither clean nor ready in case we needed it right now. See to it.'

John clicked his heels and took the gun, 'Yes Sir.' He quickly walked away, not looking back.

Sir Marsh briefly glanced at Lily. 'We are about ready to go,' he mumbled in her general direction and turned away.

Lily rose, brushing off her dress. 'Very well, so will I by the time everyone else is.' She moved past him, tired of his ever-changing attitude. Suddenly he was so cross all the time.

'You should not have done that.'

Lily turned against her better judgement. 'I beg your pardon?'

'Earlier, you should have stayed in the carriage like I told you.'

Lilliane frowned. So that was what was bothering him so much. She tried to walk away, but could not as her temper flared up instantly. 'I am not one of your soldiers Sir, you can not order me around.'

'No, you're less than that; you're a woman,' shot Sir Marsh back.

Lily bit back a reply, knowing she had already acted improper by arguing with him. 'Very well Sir, I shall keep that in mind.' Turning away from him, she added softly. 'Next time I will let them shoot you.'

Lily climbed in the carriage without saying anything else to anyone. She wanted to give Rose a break, and at the same time keep an eye on Donovan who was sitting across from Eliza and her. She let Eliza chatter on without adding anything coherent to the conversation. Her thoughts consumed her completely. Women were less than men, she knew that, but to have it thrown in her face like that and by Sir Marsh. After what she had tried to do for him. Lilliane clenched and unclenched her fist, trying to get her temper under control again. They still had a very long way to go and unfortunately Sir Marsh would be there till the very end.

Sir Marsh had given the order to go. They were going to the nearest village to see if there was a proper surgeon for Donovan. Lilliane could hardly wait for another bath. This time she would not spend one minute of the evening with either of the Marsh men.

The carriage passed through the countryside. Lily could not enjoy the scenery as she normally would. She wished she was at the castle back home, when her mother was still alive. That feeling of being home, that feeling of belonging, she had never experienced that anymore since her mother's death. Nothing had been the same.

They arrived at a most charming town. Lilliane took it all in with partial indifference. Still, the beauty of the town made her feel less gloomy than she had been feeling. By the time the carriage stopped, there was even a small smile playing on her lips. She not only had her father's temper, she also had her mother's spunk and sweetness of character.

Sir Marsh opened the carriage door. Lily ignored his offer to help her out and swiftly moved past him, with Eliza following her. The men helped Donovan to a surgeon, while the two ladies and Sir Marsh went into the inn to secure rooms for the night.

Lily was glad when the door of the room closed behind her. Blissful silence enfolded her. Eliza was downstairs ordering dinner. Lilliane sat on the edge of the bed, rubbing her hands over the bedcovers. The moment relaxed her as she tried to put everything that had happened over the past few days in perspective.

Her fifteen birthday had come and passed, she had almost forgotten about it herself, if it wasn't for Eliza's gift. The girl had woven two new handkerchiefs for her.

Eliza had almost drowned, Donovan had been wounded and, if it hadn't been for Mr Johansson, Sir Marsh would have been shot. It wasn't as if the Lieutenant had jumped up to help his brother.

Lieutenant Marsh.... Lily wondered why he had hesitated. He had a clear shot to hit Leopold; Mr Johansson had been standing further away and he had succeeded easily. She was worried about that man, worried if he was planning to do something to his brother. Or perhaps just worried what that kind of betrayal would do to him.

Sir Marsh, she could think his name again without it setting her temper aflame. She had forgiven his rudeness and arrogance, he was a man after all, and he knew better than her. Lily giggled at herself; was it Sir Marsh's stature that made her forgive him so quickly or was it the rest of him?

Snuggling down on the bed, she sighed happily. It had been an exhausting day and thinking it over again and again only made her more tired. She closed her eyes and soon fell into a pre-dinner slumber.

Eliza woke her after what seemed to her a too long nap. In her dreams she had been plagued by the events of the day, mixed with a masked man trying to poison Rose to sabotage their journey more and the Leopold character killing Sir Marsh. Lieutenant Marsh only stood there, smiling and smoking his pipe. She did not know what to make of him. Was her subconscious mind telling her that Lt. Marsh was planning something or had she let her imagination get the better of her?

As she ate the meal Eliza had served her at the table, she tried not to think about it anymore, for fear of driving herself mad. When she had enough to eat, she sent Eliza out to check on Donovan and Rose and went out herself for some air and exercise.

To get to the front door, you had to pass through the inn's drawing room, a most inconvenient design felt Lily. The drawing room was not very full. Only two or three tables had guests.

Lily paused to appreciate the music. The musician was not exemplary, but still above average. Lilliane was very fond of music, though she could not play very well. Her aunt had despised music and did not teach her anything beyond what was expected. The song finished, Lily decided to continue before she got too caught up in it again. Fresh air had been her main target after all.

Passing the last table with people, she thought she saw something familiar from the corner of her eye. She looked, blushed, and quickly looked away again. Sir Marsh was sitting at the table, accompanied by a young lady. They were talking and even laughing as if they knew each other very well.

Lilliane upped her pace. Something inside her had stirred when she saw them so cheerfully together. Sir Marsh was obviously not being cross with her. And who was this young lady? How did she end up here, in the very inn they were staying in?

10
Visitors

Lily sat on a rock, dangling her toes in the water. There was no one in the vicinity of her or the water, yet she was still close enough to the town in case she needed assistance. She had spent the last half hour contemplating the girl in the inn. Her complexion was nearly brilliant and her tiny blonde curls framed her pretty face. Even her teeth looked great in the glances she had allowed herself to take as she passed them. What was a lady like that doing in a small town inn, and what was her relationship to Sir Marsh?

Pulling her feet up, she sighed and hugged her knees. All this thinking was too much. She needed something to take her mind off things. At home she would swim in the stream, but she couldn't do that here. It wasn't even safe to be out on your own. Perhaps it was better to go back to the inn.

Lilliane was putting her shoes back on when she heard the telltale sounds of people coming. She looked up only to gasp out loud; none other than Sir Marsh and that girl were coming towards her. She could not be sure if they had seen her yet, they did not give any sign of recognition; Lily wondered if she could move passed them if she took the other way. The young lady in question looked charming in every way; where she had hair sticking out at all angles and no doubt that she looked almost wild.

As they came closer, Lily scampered around the rock. She made her way over rocks in the water, towards the other side

The Last Lord's Wife

of the bank. The stones were slippery and she almost lost her balance twice. Sir Marsh and his companion were still far enough for her to get away. She looked over her shoulder to check their progress as she stepped on the last stone. Her foot slipped off, Lily tried to keep her balance, but couldn't; she fell into the stream with a loud splash. The water was deep enough to soak her clothes; she sat up on her knees, the stream coming to her waist, and rubbed the muddy water from her face. She finished just in time to see Sir Marsh and the young woman running towards her.

'Are you okay miss…… oh Lady Lilliane?' Sir Marsh stopped dead in his tracks on one of the rocks.

'Is she alright?' the young lady called from the riverbank.

Lily stumbled to her feet. She hoped that the mud would hide some of her embarrassment. 'I can assure you Sir, I am quite alright. Let me go this way to the inn, I might catch up with you later.'

'Nonsense Milady, I cannot possibly let you go like this. They might not let you inside the inn.' He smirked at her.

Lily grew annoyed, but that quickly evaporated when he offered his arm to her. Sir Marsh made jokes about her appearance, but did not care if she left muddy stains on his clothes. He was taking care of her in his own way.

Sir Marsh helped her back to where his companion still stood. Lily did not wish to be introduced right now, but knew it could not be avoided. They both stopped in front of her. Lily waited for Sir Marsh to introduce them, the other lady had no such reserves.

She immediately took Lily in from head to toe and sent her a fake smile. 'Oh my, you must have had a terrible fright falling like that. Why, I was just telling Sir Marsh earlier I am not getting near the water. I am terribly frightened of ruining

67

my attire.' She smiled again, 'Not that you notice any of the stains on you dear.' She almost patted Lily's hand, but decided against it when she saw how dirty her hands were.

Lilliane tried to smile herself. At least if this lady's manners were not pleasing, she could dislike her appropriately. Sir Marsh had said nothing until now, but another look from Lily seemed to wake him. 'Lady Lilliane, may I introduce my cousin, Miss Mary Elliot to you. Miss Elliot, this is Lady Lilliane Gaeli of Geastwood castle.'

Lily curtsied, as Mary did the same. Civilities over, an awkward silence fell, not broken until Lily, still wet through, shivered from a cold breeze.

Sir Marsh immediately took action. 'We must get you back to the inn Milady, before you catch your death. Here, take my coat.' Before she could protest against dirtying it, Sir Marsh had taken off his coat and draped it over her shoulders. It still held heat from his body. Lily immediately felt warmer.

'But my dear Sir Marsh, your coat will be dirty. And what about you, you might get ill yourself,' cried Miss Elliot in outrage.

To Lily it sounded true enough to reach for the coat, but Sir Marsh told her not to with a quick shake of his head. 'I can assure you Miss Elliot, I am fine. It is not as cold as I thought and Lady Lilliane is in much greater risk of illness, wet as she is.'

By now they had entered the village and were almost at the inn. Miss Elliot's reply was lost over the sound of the carriages passing on the street. Lily could not care less.

They entered the inn and found Eliza sitting there. The girl immediately rose and came towards her mistress. She showed nothing but some surprise in her manner. 'I shall go and order the bathwater Milady.' Lily nodded in reply as Eliza curtsied and walked away.

Miss Elliot had taken a seat at a table and was doing her best to get Sir Marsh to join her. Lily almost smirked when she realised he was ignoring her and instead stayed where he was rooted. She looked up to his face. 'I shall make sure you will get your coat back as soon as possible. Cleaned of course.'

Sir Marsh dismissed the offer. 'It's okay, I am sure I will get it back by the time I need it again. Are you alright? You did not injure yourself back there, did you? Forgive me, I should have asked earlier.'

Lily genuinely smiled. 'I am fine Sir, thank you. I best get to my room now. It will be nice to get clean again.'

Sir Marsh nodded, yet he still stood still. Lily was unsure if he realised he was blocking her way.

'May I Sir?' she said, after a few moments of silence.

Sir Marsh looked embarrassed and quickly stepped aside. 'Oh yes, of course. Good night Milady.'

'Good night Sir,' replied Lily and left the room.

The next morning Lily went down to the breakfast room, hoping against all odds that Miss Elliot would not join. Her hope was quickly dashed away when she saw the lady in question sitting next to Sir Marsh. Miss Elliot was sitting so close, she was almost straddling Sir Marsh. Lily was repulsed by her behaviour and during breakfast of all things. At least it seemed Sir Marsh was not that comfortable either; thank the Lord for small favours.

It was not until Lily was in a throwing distance of the table, that she noticed someone else new sitting there next to Lt. Marsh and Mr Johansson. This man was certainly a gentleman; it was obvious from his manner of moving and speaking. He was dressed neatly, as if he was going to a ball, instead of just breakfast at a simple village inn. She noticed some resemblance between the two newcomers, though where Miss Elliot had fair hair and delicate features, the gentleman was darker.

Sir Marsh noticed her as soon as she entered the room and rose from his seat to beckon her over. Lily could see Miss Elliot's expression change to a neutral expression very quickly. The new gentleman seemed to scrutinize her carefully.

'And who is this charming young lady, Marsh? Have you've been holding back on me?'

'Of course not Elliot, I just haven't had a chance to introduce you yet. Lady Lilliane, this is Christopher Elliot, Mary's brother. Elliot, this is Lady Lilliane Gaeli.'

Lily smiled at the man and curtsied, he bowed his head. She then took a seat on the other side of Sir Marsh. Lieutenant Marsh was seated on her left.

'Did you manage to get all of the mud out of your hair and clothes dear?' asked Miss Elliot sweetly.

Lily's cheeks grew pink, 'Ah, yes, thank you Miss Elliot, it was removed quite easily.'

Lily took a few sips of the tea a servant had just poured her to end further enquiries about the topic. She waited for someone to change the subject and was very thankful to Mr Johansson for doing so.

Lilliane added as little to the conversation as civility allowed, even though Sir Marsh was trying his best to include her as much as he could by discussing parts of their journey so far.

When breakfast was over, the men retired to the billiard room. Lily was forced to stay behind with Mary Elliot. Luckily it did not seem as if Miss Elliot was paying any attention to her; the only one she seemed remotely interested in, besides herself and her brother, was Sir Marsh. With him and the other gentlemen away Mary entertained herself with some help from her maid.

Lily may as well be invisible. She smiled to herself, that wasn't even a bad idea. Lily opened the door and slipped out, she was halfway to her room before the door closed.

It was several minutes later when she decided to go back to the drawing room. The men would be arriving soon and her absence would not be acceptable. She re-entered to find them in almost the exact way they were when she left. Miss Elliot was standing at the window, setting off a monologue that was only interesting to her own ears. Her lady's maid, a small unattractive mouse of a girl called Libby, was her only listener.

Eliza was sitting on the other side of the room, fixing a hole in her apron and softly singing to herself. Lily smiled at the song, an old lullaby her nurse Beth always sang to get her to sleep. She must have used it with her daughter too. Eliza had a sweet voice, similar to her mother's.

Lily seated herself next to the girl. 'Have I been missed?' she asked, with a hint of a smile on her face.

'I am not sure miss. I can't be sure she notices things beyond what applies to herself.'

Lilliane stifled her laugh. 'That is too bold Eliza.'

'I apologize Miss.' replied Eliza smirking. Both knew these kind of conversations between them was only when they could not be overheard.

The men entered accompanied by loud noise. Miss Elliot's face immediately perked up. Lily's giggles intensified when Sir Marsh, not even looking at his cousin, made a beeline for her instead. Mr Johansson sat down with Miss Elliot and tried to engage her in conversation.

Sir Marsh seemed amused. 'Something worth sharing Lady Lilliane?'

'No Sir, it's only interesting to ladies.'

He raised his eyebrows seemingly still interested, but then decided to let it slide. Looking around, he made sure they could not be overheard by anyone, before leaning towards Lily. 'Can I ask you something Lady Lilliane?'

Lily grew curious, 'Of course Sir.'

His voice was almost a whisper. 'Is my cousin still looking at me?'

Lily looked at Mary Elliot seated behind Sir Marsh. He had his back towards her. 'She is having a conversation with Mr Johansson, Sir. She only glances at you occasionally.'

'Good, perhaps I can have some relief.'

'Sir?' Lily giggled.

'Miss Elliot was engaged to my brother Edmund. Our fathers set up the engagement, uncle married father's sister. I think that Mary, now that my brother is dead and I inherited his title, thinks that I will follow in all of his footsteps.'

'And you are not planning to?'

'Not in that one, no. My father was a good man Lady Lilliane, but I have no intention to marry out of anything but love. Miss Elliot would make a suitable wife, I have no doubt about it, but..'

Sir Marsh stared into Lily's eyes. She hardly dared to breathe. 'But, Sir?'

'....But my heart belongs to another.'

Blushing Lily looked away, aware that there were several other people in the room. She wanted to say something in reply, but did not know what would be appropriate enough.

Could she make her own affections known with just a few well chosen words as he had done? Before she could, Christopher Elliot asked Sir Marsh something, which resulted in the two men leaving the room. Lily decided to take Eliza with her and go for a walk. She knew the girl would leave her to her thoughts when desired and right now she needed to think. One thing she did know for sure already; when opportunity came, she would use it to tell Sir Marsh something. She would tell him he had her heart too.

11
Disclosures

It was several minutes later when Lily thought she could go back to the inn without blushing even deeper. It had been a short, but well spent walk. The redness of her cheeks could be blamed on the coldness of the weather and she felt as if she could face everyone again. A happiness she had never felt before had taken a hold of her since her conversation with Sir Marsh. She hoped that Miss Elliot and her brother would leave soon so that they could go back to travelling with their own group again It would be even better if Lt. Marsh went with his cousins, but she knew that would be pushing their luck. He simply had to be tolerated.

Lily had thought of nothing else but Sir Marsh. The way his eyes looked when he talked to her; the feeling of his skin on her own. All the feelings and thoughts she had suppressed the last few days came back to her now. Perhaps she could ask Donovan to write to their father. Surely, it did not matter to him who she wedded. Married to Sir Marsh, the thought alone made her smile. To think how fast she fell for this man and how deeply. It took most of her self-control to keep the smile off her face.

A servant opened the door for her and Eliza. Lily immediately examined the room for Sir Marsh. Her happiness deflated somewhat when she saw him talking to Mr Elliot and Mr Johansson, Miss Elliot near enough to him to be tickled by the ruffles on her gown. At least he had the decency to look uncomfortable. Scanning the rest of the room brought no better image forward; Lt. Marsh was sitting apart from them all, staring blankly ahead. Two men Lily did not know were talking on the other side. The rest of the room was empty aside from some servants. Lily lingered in the doorway.

'Oh Lady Lilliane, you are right in time, we must have your opinion on a matter of urgency.' Miss Elliot beckoned her towards them. She turned back to Sir Marsh as if she had not just spoken to Lily. 'My dear Sir Marsh, we must stay. I am sure Lady Lilliane will agree that it will offer a suitable distraction from travelling. We could all use another day of rest.' Lily did not know what the topic of conversation was, but she was quite literally, pulled into it by Mary Elliot. The lady grabbed her by the arm and forcefully pulled Lily towards Sir Marsh and the others when she noticed Lily did not intend to join them. 'Don't you agree Lady Lilliane?' cried Miss Elliot again.

Lily slowly pulled her arm away from Miss Elliot. A lot of self-restraint was needed to keep her from ridiculing Miss Elliot and her elaborate ways. She usually did not chastise others, but she had never before met someone like Miss Elliot. 'You must excuse me Miss Elliot, I am afraid I can not give you an answer; I do not know the topic.'

Christopher Elliot answered before his sister could, 'A ball Milady, the inn is having its monthly ball this evening. My sister is trying to persuade Sir Marsh to stay for it and travel further tomorrow.'

'Surely if you want to stay for another day it will not matter if we do,' replied Lily, still confused by the discussion. She didn't know where the Elliots' were going, but as it wasn't with them, it did not matter.

'But my dear lady, we are travelling with you from this point on. Did Sir Marsh not inform you about us?' Mr Elliot laughed out loud.

Sir Marsh avoided her gaze. 'We had a few surprises along the way. I must admit I failed to mention it indeed.'

An awkward silence followed this revelation. The three men did not know what to say, while Lily was adjusting to the idea of more Mary Elliot.

'The more company, the merrier; is it not Lady Lilliane?' Mr Johansson was the first to break the silence. Once again, Lily felt grateful towards him. It seemed he had the convenient knack for knowing what to say at the appropriate time.

'Yes indeed, Mr Johansson.' she replied and even managed a small smile. 'Beg you would excuse me.' She curtsied, leaving the men and Miss Elliot to their further discussions.

Lily walked to another corner of the room and sat down on the windowsill. She pretended to gaze out the window with pleasure, in hopes of having a moment to herself in the overcrowded room. The news that the Elliots were joining their travelling group spoiled the pleasure the view created. She had too much to think about to be content with anything, even with Sir Marsh. Lily closed her eyes and leaned her head against the wood.

Everything around her was hazy and seemed to become more distant from her with every step she took. She tried to cross the water to return to the inn, the water she had not noticed before. It looked shallow; she wondered if she could cross it without getting wet. Her foot touched the water and immediately submerged. She pulled it back.

A loud splashing made her turn, but there was no one behind her. The land had disappeared; only water was visible around her. It was already washing over her ankles. She instantly knew it would not take long before the water would submerge her completely. It was she who was sinking into the water. She was standing on quicksand and was sinking fast.

Her voice carried over the water, echoing on. The village she had seen earlier had disappeared. Was she alone? She could see nobody in the vicinity, yet sensed someone's presence none the less. Turning her head, she looked over her shoulder and saw no one still, then turned back only to nearly fall over from shock; where there had been only emptiness before was now filled with several people. Sir Marsh and Mary Elliot stood the furthest, side by side. Neither was looking at her, it seemed they only had eyes for each other. The Lieutenant was gazing at her in that peculiar way that was his trademark. None of the others even glanced at her. The entire travel group was there; all were ignoring her, even her brother.

She sank deeper into the muddy water. Her voice staggered periodically, discontinuing entirely after several attempts to ask for help. Nobody had even moved a centimetre. She gestured with her arms, tried to move her legs, but nothing seemed to work.

'Lady Lilliane, are you okay?' A voice not often heard broke through her slumber. She sat up and blinked her eyes several times.

'Yes, thank you Mr Johansson, I must have fallen asleep. How silly of me.'

Mr Johansson sat on the other side of the windowsill. 'I can assure you Milady, nothing you say or do can ever be labelled as silly; at least not when you compare it with another lady in this room.'

Lily rubbed her hand over her mouth to hide her smile. 'Mr Johansson, that is quite droll.'

He grinned in reply. 'I beg your pardon Milady.' He rose and bowed. 'Let's hope they don't go all the way to the capital with us,' he said softly and left her alone again.

Lily turned back to look out the window. The nightmare was quickly vaporizing from her mind. 'Let's hope indeed,' she said to herself in reply of Mr Johansson.

Though the entire building was quiet, the silence of the rooms was almost deafening to her ears. A friendly looking monk had brought her to the room her brother was currently in. The villagers that came to this monk-run infirmary were treated in the room next to the prayer-room. People of privilege resided in smaller private rooms on the second floor. It was uncommon for a woman to visit a man alone, but a short note from Sir Marsh and the knowledge that she was his sister granted Lily access to Donovan's sickroom.

The boy looked more pale than the last time she had seen him. Lily gasped at how bleak he looked. The brother in charge of the infirmary had properly bandaged his foot and a mug, with foaming herbal-tea, stood next to his bed. The room was small and, apart from a bed and one moderate-sized table, a wooden chair was the only other piece of furniture. An unlit candle had been placed by the tea, together with a window filled with golden coloured glass, it was the only source of light. A fireplace produced heat. The room was well fitted for all of Donovan's needs.

Lily moved the chair closer to the bed. Donovan was finally sleeping; he had had a restless night. She brushed some hair away from his forehead. Ball or no ball, as long as Donovan was too sick to be moved, they were not going anywhere. He had spiked a fever only the previous morning and was not doing very well.

Staying as long as she thought she could without causing talk, Lily left Donovan's bedside an hour later. It was time to dress for the ball that she did not feel like attending. It was a duty she despised today, she really wanted to stay with Donovan and nurse him back to full health. Eliza was still in their room when she opened it. The girl curtsied when she saw her mistress then continued to lay out a dress and accessories.

Lily frowned when she saw the gown Eliza had chosen for that evening. 'Eliza, that one is really too smart for a ball like this.' she sighed and sank into a chair.

'Milady, is it not good to look your best for certain company.'

Lily raised her eyebrows; 'What do you mean?'

Eliza turned back to the gown, smoothing away some wrinkles Lily could not see. 'Nothing in particular Miss.'

Lily didn't think Eliza sounded very sincere, but decided not to push further. She was not really sure she wanted to know. She washed up, dressed, and let Eliza do her hair. She had to admit she liked the result herself. Eliza had truly outdone herself and if she was honest with herself, she did want to look her best; whether it was to beat Mary Elliot at her own game or to make sure Sir Marsh didn't go the way of her nightmare, she wasn't sure.

The ballroom of the inn was packed with people by the time Lily made her entrance. Candles and oil lamps tried to outshine each other in every corner and music was playing loudly. There was a general air of cheerfulness. Lily had to admit to herself it did look quite lovely, they had not gone overboard; though the space was richly decorated, it still felt cosy and welcoming.

She searched for Sir Marsh and was disappointed to find he had not arrived yet. Mister Elliot was standing in a corner of the room. Lily wanted to turn around before he noticed her, but realised it was too late when he quickened his pace to cut her off.

'Lady Lilliane,' he bowed, 'you look very beautiful.'

She curtsied and smiled out of civility. 'Thank you Sir.'

'May I have the honour of the first two dances Milady?'

Lily was horrified; she had not planned to dance a lot, but did not want to stand up with anyone else but Sir Marsh, perhaps Mr Johansson a few times too. To have to dance with Mr Elliot instead and the first two; she knew she could not refuse him without being rude.

'Of course Sir.... except Sir Marsh asked me earlier and I am afraid I promised them to him.' she said. She hoped she could talk to Sir Marsh before his cousin caught her at her fib.

'Really? And here I thought you hadn't really talked to Marsh by yourself today.'

Lily blushed at the insinuation. She did not know what to reply. At that moment, the music volume increased, saving her from replying a bit longer, though it did not lessen her blush.

She was fidgeting with her handkerchief, convinced that her lie would be discovered, when Sir Marsh and, unfortunately, Mary Elliot and Lt Marsh joined them.

Sir Marsh greeted everyone and only looked at her oddly for a moment, before offering his arm. 'Shall we dance Milady?' he said sweetly, smiling at her.

Her blush increased, in a different manner than before. He had heard her or he simply wanted to dance with her. The reason did not matter; she would not have to dance with Mr Elliot. She nodded, placing her hand on his. He led her to the dance floor. Neither looked back, the people behind them were of no interest.

The dance began and they followed the rhythm, clasping hands or moving away from each other when it was needed. 'You look very beautiful Lady Lilliane.'

Lily smiled genuinely, 'Thank you Sir.'

Sir Marsh studied her intently, not saying anything. 'But you do not seem to be enjoying yourself fully. Is there something the matter? I mean, apart from the forced company of my cousins,' he added, winking.

'It's my brother Sir, he spiked a fever,' replied Lily. She was worried for her brother, yet could hardly keep the smile off her face; Sir Marsh already knew her quite well.

'And you want to be with him and not here... I see.' he said nothing as they continued the dance. She was not sure what he was thinking and resolved not to speak until he did again. When he continued to talk, it was by way of a subject change. Lilliane went along with it, if he did not want to discuss it further, she would not try either.

The dance over, Sir Marsh led her back to their group and left her there. Lily tried not to stare as he retreated from them without more than a pardon, instead focusing on the topic of discussion. The conversation between Mary Elliot and her brother was not interesting enough to keep her distracted. She soon found her thoughts wandering off, thinking about Sir Marsh and his hasty departure. She grew even more surprised when she saw him return, Eliza in his tow.

They stopped in front of them. 'I beg your pardon, I must borrow Lady Lilliane for the evening, she is wanted somewhere else.'

The others looked confused, but made no objection. Lily curtsied at them, before following Sir Marsh and Eliza out of the room. She was just as confused as they seemed to be, but asked nothing.

A carriage awaited them outside. Sir Marsh helped Lily and Eliza in, before climbing in as well. Lily had an inkling about their destination. She felt a happiness inside her grow with every step the horses took. They did not talk. Eliza occasionally shot her a smug look, but wisely said nothing. Lily dared not to look Sir Marsh in the eye.

They arrived at the church. The carriage stopped and Sir Marsh exited to help them both. One of the brothers brought them to Donovan's room. Sir Marsh smiled at Lily and opened the door to the room. Lily managed to smile back briefly. Donovan looked worse than earlier. He was moving in his sleep and still looked pale. Lily immediately grabbed a rag, dabbing some cold water on his forehead. Eliza made herself useful too.

Lily expected Sir Marsh to go back to the inn and was surprised when he re-entered the room with another chair for him and Eliza.

'I think I might stay a bit longer, if you don't mind. They can manage without me at the ball.'

'No, of course not. I'm grateful for the company.' She fussed over Donovan to hide her surprise. 'Sir Marsh?'

'Yes Milady?'

'Thank you. Thank you very much. I don't think they would have let me enter without your company.'

Sir Marsh smiled. 'You're welcome Milady, you're very welcome.'

12

Consequences

It was two days later when Donovan was well enough to sit up in bed again for longer periods. He had even made a few short walks through the corridor outside of his room, supported by either Sir Marsh or John. Eliza and Lily had seldom left the room at the same time. Some commitments she could not avoid; dinner, noon-meal and the occasional hour or two in the drawing room was mandatory. The minutes crept by slowly in a room alone with Mary Elliot and her maid. When she was at the inn, Eliza was always with Donovan. Only the moments with Sir Marsh were worth being away from Donovan.

They dwelled in the countryside around the inn up to an hour a day. John always accompanied them, taking the place of his sister when she couldn't. Sometimes Lily wished she could be alone with Sir Marsh, but she knew it could cause great scandal. With Mary Elliot, poking her nose around every corner, it was better not to risk it. John Marsh was scarcely in their vicinity, something Lily did not mind at all, yet it worried her too. Was he planning something or simply growing more peculiar without a solid reason? She trusted him very little and could not help but watch him for signs of trouble whenever he was near.

Mr Johansson was an entirely different story; she was appreciating him more each moment she spent with him. He was an intelligent man with a remarkable sense of humour and a quick mind. Only Sir Marsh's company was valued higher than his.

Sir Marsh…… As it often did when she was alone, her thoughts drifted to him. They had not spoken without anyone near since their dance at the ball. Or more accurately since that earlier morning. She had wanted to tell him about her own feelings, how they matched his, but they were never alone than a few minutes before someone joined. Whether it was Mary Elliot, John or Mr Johansson, the topic could not be discussed in anything but total solitude. Her heart was at stake, his too if she'd read him correctly and she was sure she did after that night spent next to Donovan's bed.

> It had been a long night guarding Donovan as he fought the fever. Eliza had fallen asleep around midnight on a straw mattress the monks had lent them. Though Lily was tired, she had not left Donovan's bedside and neither had Sir Marsh. Lily could hardly believe she was worthy of so much kindness. Sir Marsh had not returned to the ball, instead he had helped her take care of her brother, something most men would consider women's work. He worked next to her in almost silence. Did he feel responsible for Donovan's injury or did he stay because of her? She did not know, but it really did not matter.
> Donovan was drifting in and out of consciousness; Lily continually pressed a cold cloth to his forehead. She hoped it soothed him somehow, she was on edge herself. Worry for Donovan mixed with the feelings Sir Marsh

enticed. Whenever he came nearer her heartbeat accelerated.

Occasionally his fingers would touch hers when he handed her a clean cloth, or when he took the bowl of water that needed refreshing from her. Aside from the tingling feeling, she also drew comfort from his warm touch. The knowledge that he didn't have to touch her if he didn't want to filled her worried heart with happiness despite the situation.

'Perhaps you should try to catch some sleep Milady. You will wear yourself out.' Sir Marsh offered. 'I will watch over him.'

'You're very kind, Sir, but I cannot. He's my responsibility,' Lily refused with a slight shake of her head. 'But perhaps you should follow your own advice. I can take care of him by myself.'

'That I cannot do. He might be your responsibility, but you're mine Milady.' Sir Marsh looked away. 'What I mean is...'

Lily smiled, 'I know what you mean Sir, I understand.'

A small blush appeared on her cheeks when he looked at her, seemingly taking in every part of her face. 'I know you do Milady.'

Slowly she noticed him move forward. He was close enough for her to feel the warmth of his breath on her face. Would he kiss her? Should she allow it? It would not be proper, her mind told her sternly to pull away. They were in a church building. And if her aunt found out... ... How would she find out? replied her heart... She can't...

Her heart won the argument. She didn't move away, instead she waited.

What would he do? His eyes moved from her forehead to her lips and back to her eyes. His stare was intense; it almost made her look away, but she held his gaze, even as she coloured more. His breath stoked, he watched, as she seemed to be having an inner-battle with her conscience. He too had the same battle before, he didn't want her to be uncomfortable with his actions, yet he couldn't stop himself either. He needed to kiss her.

Their foreheads were almost touching. He closed the gap between them and pressed his lips to hers. They were sweet; softer even than he had imagined. He did not want to stop, but didn't want to push her too far. They were not alone, and the last thing he wanted to do was embarrass her.

After pulling away he immediately searched her eyes for signs of anger or fright, but found nothing in them that showed displeasure. He smiled.

A cough from Donovan made them turn away from each other. Lily focused on her brother and wiped the sweat from his face. She felt just as hot as her brother was. Their kiss hadn't lasted long, but it had felt as if everything had gone in slow motion.

At two in the morning Donovan's fever finally broke. Lily was tired and relieved at the same time. She sat down in a chair, closing her eyes for a few minutes, while listening to the now even breathing of her brother. She briefly registered someone stroking her cheek before falling asleep.

Donovan was recuperating, but it was taking longer than everyone had anticipated. It was not the wound that was giving the problems; it was the infection; the fever that had done the most damage. The boy needed time, more time than they had.

He banged his fist on the table in frustration. The boy was still sick, too sick for them to continue.... And that was exactly what they needed to do. His carefully constructed plan would fail if they did not progress quicker. A Lady's maid's almost drowning, delays and fevers; all things he hadn't predicted and that were inconvenient. He had wanted to slow them down a bit, but now they weren't moving at all. Perhaps it was best to get rid of some extra passengers too; they were only slowing them down.

He laughed to himself, grabbed his favourite knife and slung it towards the door. Bull's-eye, as always.

Lily draped her winter cloak around her shoulders and fastened it carefully. It was too warm for the kind of weather they were having, but she hadn't been feeling well all morning. A shiver broke free and crossed her entire back. She snuggled into the cloak, willing it to warm her quicker. Breakfast was the first order of the day, after that she would visit her brother and take Rose out for a ride. She hadn't ridden since arriving at the inn. She was looking forward to it, if only because it would help her warm up properly.

Eliza followed her down the stairs, chatting away amiably. The girl had enough reason to feel cheery; Donovan was getting better every minute, which meant that she wasn't confined to his chambers the entire day anymore. Right now John was keeping him company in place of his sister.

The door opened and Lily entered the breakfast room. Only a handful of servants occupied the room, none of the patrons were there, including her own party. Lily looked at Eliza in surprise, usually at least one of the other travellers were there. Eliza lifted her shoulders in answer; she couldn't say why the room was empty either.

Lily slid onto a chair, Eliza followed. They were now partially hidden by a large screen placed between their table and the rest; Lily thought it was nice to have some extra privacy in a large place like this. She and Eliza had just started to converse softly when louder voices came from the direction of the hall. The door flew open with a louder bang than normally, just before both the Elliots' walked in. It was clear that they were having a heated discussion by the way they were glaring at each other. Lily was unsure if they had noticed her presence in the room.

'For the last time Mary, drop it please. There is nothing either of us can do about it.'

'But surely if you asked Sir Marsh he could help and…'

'No. This is a family matter, only our own family circle should be involved. I will leave as soon as I am packed.' He scraped his throat. 'Perhaps it is best if you accompany me.'

Mary's voice turned shriller, showing her displeasure at the suggestion. 'Surely you can travel much faster without the added difficulty of myself as a travel companion brother.'

Mr Elliot nodded. 'Yes, that is true. Let's have some breakfast first and after that you can see me out.'

He moved towards their table, followed by his sister. Lily had been pretending not to hear their conversation since they entered. She talked to Eliza in a half-whisper and kept her eyes away from the siblings as much as her manners compelled her to do, but she couldn't help but overhear snatches of the conversation. Mr Elliot was leaving them for home apparently, and his sister was not going with him. Her feelings of dislike for the one did not lessen her compassion for the other; if he was departing in such a hurry it must be something dreadful.

Elliot sat down at the table, surprise on his face when he noticed the lady and her maid already there.

'Good morning Milady, early rise today?' He continued without waiting for an answer, a hint of nervousness in his manner. 'I am afraid I can not wait for the others to join us, I have to leave immediately after breakfast. Something has come up at home. I suppose you may have heard some of it as Mary and I discussed it.'

Some deception here was necessary to avoid further awkwardness. Lily replied in the negative to his inquiry, then quickly steered the subject in a different direction. 'Sir Marsh and the Lieutenant are coming for breakfast,' she said, gesturing in their direction.

Mr Elliot rose to meet them halfway, saying something in a low whisper to his cousins. Sir Marsh nodded in understanding then resumed his course to the table.

'Good morning Milady, Miss Elliot.' He bowed his head to both. 'I just came back from seeing Donovan. He has recovered enough to travel. We will be leaving again shortly after noon.'

Lily took this information in as Mary Elliot started a conversation with Sir Marsh. They were continuing their journey, part of her was sad because it meant less private moments with Sir Marsh, but she was definitely happy that her brother was doing well. With a smile on her face, she joined in the conversation.

13
Storm

They had been driving in the carriage for some time now. Lily dozed in and out of sleep. Even the constant chattering of Mary Elliot could not keep her awake. The past few days seemed to be a combination of a dream and a nightmare. She looked next to her and smiled. Donovan had his head against the side of the carriage; he seemed a million miles away with his thoughts. The boy was still too weak to ride a horse and was confined to the carriage for now. Lily accompanied him. Being cooped up with Miss Elliot for hours at a time would be too much for him.

The carriage slowed and Lieutenant Marsh guided his horse next to it. He fumbled for the door handle, squinting his eyes. Lily wondered if he was drunk. Finally he succeeded in opening the door and backed away. They exited the carriage. Lily was pleased when Sir Marsh came up to help her brother out then came back for her. He did not return to help his cousin.

Sir Marsh led her and Donovan to an open spot where the soldiers were already setting up for their afternoon meal and break. Lily lowered herself on a plaid, thankful for the break after sitting in basically the same position in the rocking carriage. Donovan and Sir Marsh flanked her on either side.

'Have you seen this, sister?' her brother asked, in between bites of his bread. 'It is a letter from our father, delivered by courier just before we left the inn this morning.' He held the sheet out to her.

> *Dear Son,*
> *I hope to find you better than what was reported to us in your previous letter. I have sent out several of my soldiers to look for the leader of the men that attacked you. So far we have no leads; his men are not of the talking kind either. Please be sure that they will be punished for what they did to you.*
> *I hope your improved health will mean a speedy arrival at the capital. Lilliane's presence is required at the convent before the winter begins..*
> *Mother and Frederick send their greetings.*
> *Your Father,*
> *Lord Frederick Gaeli, Geastwood Castle.*

Lily handed the letter back without commenting on the contents, thanking her brother for sharing it with her. Her parents were clearly worried…. about Donovan. She had been mentioned in one sentence only. One entire sentence.

She wished they cared more about her, but was not going to let those melancholy thoughts ruin her mood. There were more than enough people who cared for her the way she was supposed to be cared for. As if reading her thoughts, Sir Marsh softly touched her shoulder blade with his hand. He rubbed it twice then quickly dropped his hand as if nothing had happened. Lily felt the heat of his hand linger and smiled inconspicuously. They had a secret that no one else knew but them, it was theirs to keep and cherish.

Miss Elliot was talking loudly to the Lieutenant, giving Lily the chance to quietly converse with her brother. 'How did you get this Donovan?'

'I told you, it was delivered through courier this morning. Lt. Marsh was the one to take the letters from the clerk. He then gave Father's letter to me.'

'There was more than one letter?' Lily's interest was piqued.

'Yes, there was a letter for Mr Elliot too. I suppose it's why he took off for his home.' Donovan took a swig from his drink and bit off a piece of meat. On his other side Mr Johansson asked him something; the boy turned his back towards his sister. Lily didn't mind, she was done with the subject herself. She took a sip of tea and concentrated on other things for the rest of the meal.

Lily nestled into her cloak, trying to shield herself from the relentless rain pouring down on them all. The wind wasn't making things easier either. The storm had come on so quickly, they were not prepared for it at all. Rose hesitated, tilting her nose towards the side.

They were moving through a heavy grown terrain and the wind kept the branches of the surrounding trees moving in all directions. They scraped the coating of the carriage as it slowly moved forward. Lily could see Eliza looking out of the window. The girl was obviously scared. This wasn't just a quick Spring-shower, this was a full-blown storm.

Sir Marsh was riding ahead, trying to find a settlement large enough for all of them to take shelter. It almost seemed as if they were in no man's land. Lily hadn't spotted a farm or house for several miles. Rose whinnied, taking a step back from a particularly large tree. Lily tried reassuring the mare by stroking, but she wasn't feeling at ease herself. Part of her wished she had done what Sir Marsh wanted her to do; sometimes she was just too stubborn for her own good.

The storm had started as a soft drizzle. Lily had been riding Rose for the last hour or so. A large part of wilderness was coming up and it was better if all horses were led by a rider and not guided while passing through. Still, she wished she was in the carriage when the rain started. Sir Marsh slowed his horse and looked at her in seriousness.

'Perhaps you should go into the carriage Milady,' he half shouted to be heard over the storm.

Lilliane pointedly shook her head, thought she detested riding in the rain. She didn't want to leave Rose. 'Thank you Sir, I am fine.' She tried smiling but it came out forced.

Sir Marsh said nothing, gave her a semi-cross look and rode to the front of the party. He had not spoken a word to her since.

Was he cross because she hadn't obeyed? Right now she didn't care; all she cared about was Rose. The mare was getting more difficult to handle every minute. If the storm didn't taper down soon or if they couldn't find shelter… She didn't think Rose could handle much more.

They rounded a corner in the road. Lily urged Rose to go further. Thunder rumbled the sky. The clouds had covered the sun and its rays completely; it almost seemed as if dusk was already approaching. The wind rustled the branches full with leaves together and back to their original places again. A loud bang was followed by lightning ahead; it hit a nearby tree and instantly caught fire. Rose whinnied loudly then rose on her hind legs, kicking her front in a wild frenzy of fear.

'Easy Rose, easy,' yelled Lily, holding on to the reins. Rose lowered back on her front legs, only to rise once again and whinnying even louder. Lily clenched her legs together, trying with all her might to not fall off.

'Easy Rose,' her voice quivered in fright as the horse worked up a fury.

'Easy.' Sir Marsh was beside her and put one arm around her waist. He pulled her off her horse with one quick movement and rode several yards away before lowering her to the ground. Lily staggered on her feet, holding onto Sir Marsh's horse. She turned back to where Rose still was. The four soldiers and Mister Johansson had managed to calm the mare down, by pulling her far away from the fire. They had all moved away from the smouldering tree. The ever-going rain had quickly put out the flames.

Lily looked at Sir Marsh. He had dismounted his horse and was standing before her. 'Are you injured Milady?'

She quickly shook her head, not sure how to work her voice. His tone only made her feel more ashamed of her earlier refusal. 'We can not stay here in the rain, we must go on. You should go into the carriage. My men will take care of Rose, not to worry.' He quickly led her to the carriage, helping her up.

She turned before opening the door, 'Thank you Sir.'

He smiled softly, 'I would say anytime, but I would rather not do that again.' Lily smiled in return and went into the carriage. As Eliza fussed over her, she answered the questions her brother and Mary Elliot fired on her. Though the feelings of fright had not entirely melted away, she was already feeling much better. Sir Marsh coming to her aid had instantly soothed her to her very core.

14
Shelter

Another log was placed on the blazing fire. Lily sighed with contentment as the heat warmed her hastily thrown on attire. They had been lucky; they had found a small farmhouse that took in travellers on the side. The soldiers and Lieutenant Marsh were sleeping in the stables, keeping the horses company as ordered by Sir Marsh. The boys were sleeping on the floor of the two men's rooms. None, Lily felt, had it so difficult as she had.

Her room was by far the biggest and the beds were quite comfortable. There were even some adjustments made especially for ladies. All in all a most pleasant room...... which she had to share with Mary Elliot. The farmhouse had no more rooms available, the storm had taken advantage of a neglected hole in the roof and several of the rooms had water damage. They were lucky to get the rooms they had now. She knew that.

Resignation was part of her nature and she had accepted the accommodation without a fuss, after all they would only be there one night. They had gone to bed, Eliza on a cot close by, but Lily could not sleep despite being rather tired. Mary Elliot's snoring was too much to bear; neither she nor Eliza could get used to the sound. She rather wondered how Libby could sleep through it at all. After tossing and turning close to an hour, Lily could bear it no longer. She exchanged her nightclothes for her dress and quietly snuck down the stairs, into the drawing room.

Eliza had followed her wordlessly. She had taken a seat slightly away from the fire, in a more secluded, and darkened corner of the room. It had not taken Eliza long to fall asleep. Lily did not think she could do it; to sleep almost upright in a chair, but the girl had no trouble with it. She looked quite content all snuggled up in her mother's quilt.

For Lily it was getting harder to keep her eyes open, perhaps it was time to go back to the room and try to tolerate Miss Elliot's snoring again. She was debating on whether or not to go, and to wake Eliza, when a sound coming from outside drew her attention.

'Not another night-wanderer.' mumbled Lily, but went to a window none the less.

It was opened to some extent to let in some fresh air. All of the windows were boarded up because of the earlier storm, but this window's hatchet had been blown off before it could be closed and there had been no time to repair it before the storm grew to its fullest.

What she saw made no sense at all; two men standing together. One was obviously upset with the other; he was gesturing wildly with his arms and shouting incoherent words Lily could not hear. She soon grew tired of watching them. It was too late at night to care for, what she thought was, two soldiers arguing. She had recognised the attire of one, but could not see his face, the other she did not think she knew at all. His clothes were definitely not recognisable.

Lilliane retook her seat in front of the fire. She closed her eyes and inhaled deeply. What would two men be doing out at this hour anyway? Something peculiar was going on in their travel-group. The flames danced around the wood, letting her mind drift off to other things. It wasn't long before sleep overtook her.

Lily slowly opened her eyes, blinking rapidly when the harsh light of the morning sun shone directly into her face. She covered her eyes and frowned, it could not be time to rise yet, what had woken her so sudden? A loud sob made her look around.

Eliza was sitting in the chair she had slept in. She had pulled her feet up and had her quilt wrapped around her. Tear streaks were evident on her face.

Rising Lily walked towards her and put her hand on the sobbing girl's arm. Eliza flinched from the sudden contact. 'Eliza, what's the matter?'

Eliza rubbed her eyes with her hands and straightened herself. 'Nothing Miss, I'm sorry to have woken you Miss.'

Lily frowned at the obvious lie. 'It can't be nothing if it has upset you so.'

'It is truly nothing Miss.' She resolutely shook her head, 'I am a bit homesick I guess.'

A servant entered the room, surprised to see Lily and her maid there already at the early hour. He offered a low bow then continued on his way.

Eliza jumped up from her chair as if bitten. 'I shall prepare your things for today Miss, excuse me.' Not waiting for a reply, she hurriedly left the room.

Lily followed her out of the room. By the time she had entered the hall, Eliza was already rounding the corner upstairs. Whatever was going on with her, it was obvious she did not want to tell. Lily was sure she knew her well enough to know that this wasn't something as simple as homesickness. Eliza had become terrified about something, or was it someone?

It was an hour later when Lily, joined by Sir Marsh, Lt. Marsh and Mr Johansson, made her way downstairs before breakfast. Miss Eliot was still in bed, resting. She had caught a violent cold the night before and felt herself too ill to eat downstairs. Libby was waiting on her hand and foot, bringing her everything. Lily had fled the room, barely able to keep her countenance. What Miss Elliot called a violent cold was nothing more than a slight case of the sniffles. The lady had barely sneezed over three times in the period that Lily was in the room. Lilliane didn't mind though, a meal without Mary Elliot was always a delightful event on itself.

Before they had reached the end of the stairs, the boy that worked the stables ran inside. 'Sir, Sir. You must come Sir.'

Sir Marsh held his hands up, 'Calm down boy, what is the matter?'

The boy inhaled deeply, out of breath from running. 'Your horses Sir, they have broken free.'

'What?'

'I swear Sir, I saw it for myself.'

'Show us,' demanded Sir Marsh, 'You better stay inside Milady, this could take a while. Best to start breakfast.'

He did not wait for an answer, as he quickly followed the boy outside. His men accompanied him. In seconds, Eliza and Lily were the only ones left. Lily was curious to see what was going on but knew that she had to obey Sir Marsh and entered the breakfast-parlour. It would be a dull meal, waiting for news to come and a nearly mute companion. Eliza had barely spoken more than three words, though she had calmed down, her general demeanour had not.

Lily finished breakfast, sitting back at the table. The shouting was still going on outside, mixed with the sound of horses in distress. She was dying to go outside and see what was amiss, but wasn't willing to risk Sir Marsh's temper for anything. She was sure the stable boy had overreacted anyway; Sir Marsh would have it under control. There was nothing else to do but wait. It was best to do that in the parlour. Perhaps she could read a bit to make the waiting less tedious. Lily rose from the table, but before she could open the door it was opened from the other side.

Libby curtsied. 'Excuse me Milady, Miss Elliot requests you keep her company in her room upstairs.'

Lily opened her mouth then closed it again. She wanted to make an excuse but could not think of a good one. 'Very well Libby, I will,' she answered reluctantly, before following Libby upstairs. All she could hope for was that the commotion outside would be resolved quickly or that someone needed her before Miss Elliot drove her crazy.

15
Reveal

'What a foolish girl, do you not agree Eliza?'

Lily looked at her maid and was not surprised to see the girl stare off into space. She would be amused if it wasn't becoming so tedious. 'Eliza, I realise Mary Elliot isn't that fascinating, but now that we have left the room you do not have a good excuse to let your mind wander off again.' She had said it with an undertone of mirth, but there wasn't even a hint of a smile on the girl's face. Lily touched her hand and Eliza jumped again. 'Eliza, please tell me what's wrong.'

For the first time that day, their eyes locked. Though Eliza remained silent, her eyes spoke of fear. Fleetingly, it looked like she wanted to say something, but then a look of resolution came over her. 'I beg your pardon Madam, I'm feeling ill, may I be excused for an hour? I shall be more myself after some rest.'

'Very well.'

Lily sighed and ran a hand over her dress. It was obvious that she did not want to confide and her skittish behaviour was getting on Lily's own nerves and she could use a moment alone herself.

After having followed Libby upstairs, Lilliane had sat next to Miss Elliot's bed while the former questioned her about the uproar outside. Libby had spied out the window earlier, she had seen that some of their horses ran off, but could not tell what was going on with certainty or if Rose was among the runaways. Several of the men came out of the stable, leading the other horses out. There was smoke coming from the inside of the stables and many of the servants ran to and forth with buckets of water.

Lily was anxious to know if anyone was hurt. The constant chattering and moaning of Mary Elliot was not making the waiting any easier. Others were trying to capture the escaped animals. Lily wanted to press her own face against the window if she couldn't go outside, but restrained herself. It was not proper; it wasn't even acceptable for Eliza or Libby to act that way. She wasn't worried about Eliza, her maid always behaved in the most proper ways.

Finally, it seemed that Miss Elliot was growing tired. With a casual wave of her hand towards Libby, the maid quickly ushered Lily and Eliza out of the room. If she wasn't so glad to leave, she would have definitely reminded Mary Elliot that this was her room too. Instead, she left with a goodbye, before Miss Elliot had the time to change her mind and call them back.

Alone, now that Eliza had left her, Lily paced the room in front of the fire. She was starting to get very testy with the inconsiderateness of Sir Marsh and the other men. Surely they would realise that she was stuck inside, not only that, she knew nothing beyond what she had heard. What if Rose had been hurt? What did the smoke mean? Was there a fire?

Her pacing intensified. She went towards the door, hesitated again and went back to pacing. If she gave in now, she would be no better than Mary Elliot and her snooping maid. She had to trust that Sir Marsh would soon inform her.

The front door opened and loud voices filled the hallway. Lily took a seat, trying to look calm, but her fidgeting hands betrayed her state of mind.

'Good work men, go clean up and then we'll meet back here to eat.'

The door was opened and Sir Marsh stepped in. All her earlier feelings of resentment vanished as she took in his appearance. He had black spots on his clothes, arms and face, probably ashes, realised Lily. There was a tear in his shirt the size of her hand and through the tears, she could see a cut in the flesh that was bleeding. Would this man ever learn to be careful? Lily thought she knew the definite answer and it did not please her much.

'What happened? Are you hurt? How are the horses? Was there a fire?' Her questions followed each other quickly, giving him no time to answer.

Sir Marsh held up his hands, he smiled. 'Calm down Milady, we are all fine and so are most of the horses. Two of them had the edges of their tails singed, but the others are fine apart from some troubled nerves. Someone left a burning pipe near some hay. It caught fire rather quickly, we were lucky some of the horses got out by themselves or we may not have caught wind until it was too late.' Sir Marsh rang the bell for a servant and asked for some tea and food to be served in the parlour. 'If you will excuse me Milady, I have no desire to leave a black mark on the furniture.'

He went upstairs to change clothes and wash himself. Lily made him promise to let her look at the cut in his arm later before she would agree to let him go at all. He willingly consented.

The men came downstairs; washed, and clean shaven. Lily listened to their story about the fire and was relieved that no animal or person had gotten seriously hurt. A few bumps and bruises was all that was reported, from walking around in the dark and smoky stables. It was confirmed it had been a pipe, but since it was burned almost beyond recognition, there would be no luck in discovering the owner. It was thought highly unlikely that the guilty person would step forward to claim almost burning down a stable.

'There, that feels better, doesn't it Rose.' Lily slowly guided the brush over the horse's back, removing some of the debris and ashes. The mare was unharmed in every other way and had calmed down considerably since Lily had entered. The barn was temporarily converted into a stable until the real stables were cleaned and repaired. Lily was taking care of Rose while the men ate. Sir Marsh had agreed, but only if she would accompany him on a ride through the countryside later. They were leaving the next morning, since Miss Elliot was sure she could not ride in the state she was in. Her nerves had taken a toll because of the confusion of the morning and her cold was going strong as well. There was no possibility to go further now.

'My dear lady, you're riding in the carriage. One could hardly call that exhausting,' said Lieutenant Marsh to his cousin.

Miss Elliot looked quite insulted and was about to say something unbecoming, when Sir Marsh put an end to the dispute by settling the matter; they were leaving at dawn, no matter what was happening.

Lily patted the mare. She had finished brushing her; the stable boy would clean up and prepare Rose for her ride with Sir Marsh. John would accompany them, as Eliza was no horsewoman. She left the barn just in time to see Sir Marsh coming her way from the house, followed by John.

'Are you ready for our ride Milady?' he asked, smiling.

She echoed his smile. 'Yes Sir, Rose is already being saddled.'

'Good, I will check if our horses are ready as well.' He bowed his head and left her.

Lily watched him leave. The stable boy came out leading Rose; she went to the mare and waited for Sir Marsh to come out.

With every step they took away from the farmhouse, the spirits of both got brighter. They were happy to be in each other's company. Sir Marsh made jokes that amused Lily greatly, John kept his horse somewhat behind them, far enough to keep their conversation private, but near enough in case his mistress needed him. Lily was glad the boy was so discreet. They rode at a normal pace, enjoying the countryside and one another's presence. Lily noticed that, though Sir Marsh was keeping up a light conversation and doing his best to amuse her, there were times when he seemed absentminded, his thoughts miles away, almost as if he would rather be silent. She attributed most to the events of the morning. His horse Andiamo was one of two horses' whose tail was slightly singed. Beyond that, the stallion was fine.

It was in one of those moments of silence, when he kept looking in her direction every few minutes. She found it unnerving, though she wasn't sure why. He had often looked at her before. They arrived at a meadow. A beautiful field full of flowers and grass, with a man-made path crossing it towards a stream. Willows were scattered around the side of the water.

'It's beautiful here,' said Lily, breaking the silence.

Sir Marsh halted his horse slowly. 'Indeed it is. This is a nice place to talk a walk, is it not Milady. John can stay with the horses. We will stay in sight of him and make sure we can see him as well.'

Lily nodded and smiled. 'Sounds like a plan.'

She stopped Rose and dismounted, tying the horse to a tree. Sir Marsh did the same with Andiamo. John came up to them and halted his horse.

'We are going to take a walk, wait here,' said Sir Marsh. John nodded, dismounted, and, after securing his horse, made himself comfortable against the tree. He could see most of the meadow from there, as they were standing on a hill.

Sir Marsh and Lilliane began their descent down the hill. Lily looked around, taking in the scenery. She breathed in deeply. It was nice to stretch her legs after the ride. Sir Marsh was quiet, his gaze on something far away. Lily was unsure if he was looking at something in the distance, or something in his mind. She did not want to ask.

At long last he looked at her, still not speaking. Several times, he opened and closed his lips, unsure on how to begin speaking. 'Miss Lily…. I mean, Lady Lilliane…'

Lily smiled, trying to reassure him to continue, 'Lily is fine when we are without company.'

Some of his natural confidence reappeared in his manners. 'Only if you call me William.'

Averting her eyes, Lily blushed. 'Alright… William.'

The silence almost consumed them again, when Sir Marsh went back to his previous state of pondering.

'Lily.' He halted and half turned to her. All cheerfulness was gone from his face. 'I want you to know that, no matter what I have to tell you today, I love you. I don't mean to… I mean, I didn't plan to fall for you as much as I did, but now that I have…'

Lily looked at him alarmed. His uncertain demeanour was beginning to scare her. 'What is it Sir?'

He took a deep breath then resumed walking. 'What do you know about the war?'

'The war?' She was unsure of his motives for asking.

'Yes.'

'The King declared war on our neighbour in the West after they killed the Queen. Her Majesty was on a family-visit to her brother, the King of our neighbour, and he killed her to get revenge on our King.

All young men should prepare themselves for battle, though it is unsure when the actual fighting will commence.'

Sir Marsh nodded, 'Many of our people are rumoured to favour our neighbour's ruler. It is why there are so many soldiers scouting our country's roads.'

'Like the men that checked our papers the other day.'

'Yes, exactly.' He scratched his chin, wondering how to go on. 'The Queen died without children. The King has no heir.' Sir Marsh looked at her directly, 'The King has ordered nobility across the country to send their maiden daughters to the capital. He will pick one to wed; the others will most likely be his concubines. It is why your father took me into his service.'

Lily stopped cold, 'My father? What does he have to do with the King…. Unless… the soldier, he knew, didn't he? And you knew too, but you didn't tell me. The soldier realised it yet you said nothing to me.' She was getting angrier with every second she thought about it more, 'How could you kiss me. How could you let me feel this way when you knew all along I am as good as betrothed.'

'My dear Lilliane... Lily, did you think I wanted you to feel like this. I certainly did not anticipate falling for you either, but I did. I love you Milady.'

Lily closed her eyes for a moment, savouring the words as she had done before. For a full minute, she pretended that nothing mattered but the love they felt for each other, but when she opened her eyes again it all came back in threefold. She saw him standing before her, as he had often done in their days of travels. She had been mad at him, worried for him, had laughed with him... There was no doubt she cared deeply for this man, despite their short acquaintance, but it seemed that it was not meant to be.

'It does not matter Sir, how we feel. I cannot disobey my father; it is clear what he wants my path to be. I can not disobey our King either.' She took a step back from him and swallowed. A heavy lump had formed in her throat, making it difficult to breathe. 'I think we should keep our distance from now on.'

Her voice sounded more secure than she felt. She wasn't sure what she wanted him to say, but did not dare to meet his eyes.

'Very well Milady.' Sir Marsh turned abruptly away from her and started to walk back to the horses.

She could not keep herself from calling out once. 'Sir Marsh.' He half turned, his body stiff. She knew he was hurting too. 'I do love you.' He only nodded then continued to walk away.

Lily covered her mouth with her hand to keep herself from calling him back a second time. She didn't know what she could say to make it better. It wasn't fair that her father had not informed her about his decision, nor that she could not explain it to Sir Marsh in a manner that would take his pain away. It probably did not matter; she knew she had hurt him in a way that could not be repaired.

And perhaps, as she thought of what awaited her in the capital, that was for the best.

16
Chances

The silence on the way back was very different than before. This one was uncomfortable, with an air of accusations lingering on the edges. Lily kept still. John was her companion now; Sir Marsh was riding ahead of them. The boy knew nothing of their conversation, whether he had picked up snatches she could not say, he did not mention a single word. Always the good servant. Duty, honour, protocol, it ran through their lives as a thick red thread, keeping every part connected.

She was having trouble accepting what he had told her. Married to the King? Sure, their ruler had a reputation for being a fair King, taking good care of all his people, but if you read between the lines you would understand that he was also cruel to the people that lived with him. He was selfish, impatient, and easily bored. A most difficult man to live with. She thought it very unappetising that he, of all men, would become her lord and master.

They arrived at the farmhouse. Sir Marsh gave his horse to a servant, and, after a quick bow towards her, went inside even before she had dismounted Rose. She could understand his feelings; of course he had reason to be distraught, but that didn't mean it was her fault. She dismounted, and distractedly patted Rose on her back, before handing the reins to John. Hopefully Mary Elliot was either asleep or out of the room, because the only thing she wanted to do was lie down on her bed and sleep. Perhaps, if she would wake up later, it would have all turned out to be one big nightmare.

She was having no luck today. Mary Elliot was awake, sitting up in her bed and quite alone. Her lady's maid was arranging her food; she had been alone for almost ten whole minutes and was rapidly becoming very bored.

'Oh Lady Lilliane,' she said in a high-pitched squeal when Lily had carefully opened the door. 'I'm in desperate need of some entertainment. Come.' She patted the bed. 'And tell me where you ran off to this morning. I glanced out the window and saw you and my dear cousin William Marsh ride off.'

Lily noticed her pupils dilate and saw her nose flare up. She realised Miss Elliot had spied on them earlier and was very eager for information. Ignoring the invite to come closer and sit on her bed, Lily made her way over to her own cot instead and pretended to look for something in her bag. 'We went for a short ride, quite uneventful. I've had a dreadful headache for most of the morning, so I cut the trip short.' Lily sat down on the bed and tried to smile to her temporary roommate. 'Like I said, quite uneventful.' Whether Mary Elliot believed her, she did not mind or care; what was Miss Elliot to her. Absolutely nothing.

Libby arrived with food, distracting Miss Elliot long enough for Lily to lay down and turn her back towards the others, but the exclaims and cries from Miss Elliot and her maid soon made it impossible to stay even a minute longer. She quickly curtsied, and shut the door behind her before Mary Elliot had the chance to interrogate her again.

It had been a stroke of real luck; the first one she had had all day. As she exited the bedroom she had turned around and bumped into Eliza. The girl had just been coming around the corner.

'Oh Eliza, where have you been?' exclaimed Lily.

'I beg your pardon Miss; I was just coming to see you. I've found something that will make this evening more tolerable than last night.'

Lily's interest was piqued. 'What is it?'

'It's best if I show you Miss.' Eliza turned and walked back in the direction she had come from. Lily followed her to the other end of the corridor, where the girl opened a door.

The room was small, much smaller than any of the other rooms she had seen in the house. It had a bed and one dresser. Lily walked into the room, stopping next to the window. Though the furniture was nothing out of the ordinary, the amount of light the window afforded and the view made the room quite adequate for their last night here.

'A most pleasant room, is it not.' said Eliza, smiling for the first time in Lily's presence that day. 'A servant told me about it and showed it to me. He had already asked his master's permission, we are free to use it for the night. That is, if you rather not spend another night with Miss Elliot.'

Lily patted her playfully on her hand and laughed. 'No thank you, I think this will do quite nicely. If you'll collect our things from the other room…'

Eliza nodded and curtsied. Lily felt sorry that the girl had to deal with Mary Elliot again, but was in no mood to do it herself. She lay on the bed, kicking off her shoes. At home, she would never have done that. If her aunt found her handling her things in that manner, there would be trouble, but right now she felt like doing something against protocol. Since she wasn't prone to do anything huge that would dishonour herself and her family, something little had to do.

Lying back on the pillow, she stared at the ceiling, trying to clear her mind. It was no use, no matter what she thought of, she kept coming back to Sir Marsh. With a sigh, she rolled onto her side and closed her eyes. Despite the troubled state of her mind, she fell asleep long before Eliza returned.

Slowly opening her eyes, Lily stretched her arms and raised herself on her elbows. For a moment, she was disoriented, until she recognised the small room Eliza had discovered. The maid was a foot away, working on some sewing.

'Did you have a nice rest Miss?'

Lilliane nodded, 'Yes, thank you Eliza. Did I sleep long?'

'No Miss, only an hour or two. Dinner is in two hours.' She smiled. 'I would have roused you soon if you hadn't woken. I expect you want to look your best for certain company.' said Eliza, almost winking at her.

Lily looked away, not responding. Eliza didn't know how that hurt her; how could she.

'Did I say something wrong Miss?' asked Eliza alarmed.

Lily pushed the fresh tears away and forced herself to face her maid. 'No, of course not, everything is fine. Normal evening attire will do. There is no-one special here.'

Eliza frowned, but kept her lips shut. The girl was often her confidante, and she would be in this matter too, but not yet. It was all too new to talk about it with anyone. To say it out loud would make it real. Lily still wasn't ready for that.

About an hour and a half later, at the common time to go downstairs, Lily descended the stairs to join their party for dinner. She was feeling nervous; she had barely seen Sir Marsh since that morning and would now be spending several hours in his company again. It was fortunate that they would not be alone, though she wasn't sure if company was such a good idea either. How would he act? She was determined to be civil, even if he was not. She did not want to tell the whole world their affairs, especially not people prone to gossiping like Miss Elliot.

The servant opened the door to the parlour for Lily. She nodded at him, and entered, expecting the room to be occupied with people, but the room was almost entirely empty…. except for Sir Marsh. Lily hesitated, wondering where everyone was. Sir Marsh rose and looked at her.

'Good evening Milady, I'm afraid it's just the two of us for dinner. Miss Elliot is still in bed. Mr Johansson went to the next town over and my brother is out scouting with my men.' When Lily still did not budge, he moved towards the door. 'If you want, I can let you be.'

This woke Lily from her reverie, 'No, it's fine. I just didn't expect it, that's all.' Both fell silent, avoiding each others gazes at much as possible.

A servant told them dinner was ready and they trailed him to the dining room. Sir Marsh followed Lily closely. When they stopped to let the servant open the door, he quickly leaned forward and whispered next to Lily's ear, 'I swear to you; I did not plan this.'

Lily blushed but did not have to time to answer. Only yesterday she would have loved having dinner with just him; how quickly some things changed.

They ate and drank their dinner without tasting much of anything. Certain topics were banned from conversation, it was painfully difficult to keep up the small talk, but Lily was determined to do it at any cost. Perhaps, she thought, as she looked at how Sir Marsh drifted off into thought, it was why it was so hard. How could they make it easier for themselves; for each other? Lily tried to keep her mind on the present; it was probably not the best time to let her thoughts wander. Easier said then done though as Sir Marsh hardly seemed to try at all.

After a particularly long silence, where neither had said more than two words together, Lily sighed and put her utensils down. She gave the one servant present a motion to leave them and turned to Sir Marsh as soon as they were alone. He looked at her in question.

'Really Sir, can we not get past this. This is not making either of us very happy. We still have quite a trip to go, which will seem three times as long if we can't even be civil to each other.' She pressed her lips together, knowing fully well she had spoken rather too boldly to him, yet again.

Sir Marsh did not seem upset about her tone; he stared at her intensely for a long moment, before nodding in agreement. 'You are right Milady, I apologize.' Sir Marsh smiled at her.

Despite her resolution, Lily felt her feelings deepen with every second of eye contact. Regretfully, she looked away and picked her utensils up again. They finished their dinner still not saying much, but at least the awkwardness had disappeared for now.

17

Acquaintances

Lily woke at dawn and rose quickly. Eliza was already packing their things away in a hurried manner. Their journey would be continued directly after breakfast, which was earlier today than usual. Sir Marsh wanted to make up for lost time. A lot of lost time. He had mentioned it to her the previous day and Lily agreed with him. They had added several days to their trip. It was better for all, especially for Sir Marsh and herself, if they concluded their travels soon. Better for Sir Marsh if she was no longer in his immediate surroundings. About her own future in the capital she cared very little, her fate was sealed whether she was happy about it or not, but she did not want Sir Marsh to suffer anymore. He had not asked for these feelings, all he had done was accept an assignment to bring a Lord's daughter to the capital.

After dressing, she went downstairs, meeting Mr Johansson in the hallway. She supposed he had come back late the previous night, for she had not seen him at dinner or the hours after that. She curtsied and smiled shyly. Something in his manner had changed though she didn't know what. He looked very serious, more so than she had seen before. His demeanour changed when he saw her; he smiled too, but not as brightly as she was used to.

'Good morning Sir.' she said softly.

'Good morning Milady. I hope you are well?'

'I am, thank you.' A little deceit was necessary, as she had no intention on telling all to him. 'And you too I hope,' she added out of politeness. She sensed he was not in the mood for conversing beyond the ceremonial greeting.

He answered distracted, 'Yes, thank you,' and then accelerated his pace when he saw one of the soldiers standing in the downstairs hall. 'Excuse me Milady. Peterson. Can I have a word?' The two men went outside together; Lily continued into the breakfast parlour.

Mary Elliot and Lieutenant Marsh were already seated. Sir Marsh was standing at a nearby window, staring out through it. Miss Elliot was talking to the Lieutenant non-stop, either not caring or noticing that he wasn't paying attention. Lily sat down across from the pair, forcing herself not to glance at Sir Marsh constantly. The less she would interfere in his affairs from now on, the better for them both.

Mr Johansson soon joined them, sitting next to Lily. It was pleasant and vexing at the same time. Her heart only wanted one man to sit next to her; the same man her head told her to forget. At least this time the decision was made for her by another. They ate breakfast with Mary Elliot doing most of the talking. None of the men seemed to be in the mood for much conversation. Lily tried her best to be polite and keep up her end of the tête-à-tête. When breakfast was over, everyone escaped outside, to prepare their horses and to get themselves ready for the day's travels.

They had been riding for almost two and a half hours; it was nearing their midday break. Lily alternated riding next to Sir Marsh and Mr Johansson. It would seem odd if she suddenly avoided him entirely, and he was still the most agreeable person of the group to ride next to. Mr Johansson was telling an amusing story, with Lily only paying attention at intervals. Her mind was too engaged with different matters.

Just before departing, one of the soldiers had come up to Sir Marsh. Lily had been lucky enough to hear snatches. One of the reins, the last spare according to the soldier, was in two pieces. If one broke while they were travelling, it could cause great inconvenience, not to mention once again it would mean a delay. Sir Marsh had examined the leather closely, before walking away without another word. He had not mentioned anything about it since.

It was odd for Lily too. Why would a strap like that break while it wasn't in use? It hadn't been moved from its place since they had arrived at the farmhouse and there was no report of it being broken then. It was almost as if they were being.... sabotaged... but why? And who would do such a thing?

Her first guess was Lieutenant Marsh, but she could not think of a motive for him. She briefly thought of Sir Marsh himself but immediately scolded herself. Of course he wouldn't do that. What could be gained from delaying his own travels? Mr Johansson? Again no motive. Miss Elliot? Lily couldn't imagine a lady lowering herself to do something like that. One of the soldiers perhaps? Except for Robert Pike, she could see them all doing that, but yet again she could think of no motive. Lily sighed to herself, putting it out of her mind. Guilty or not, perhaps it was necessary to keep a closer eye on Lieutenant Marsh, if only to make sure he wouldn't be responsible for the next weird occurrence.

She took a bite of bread and chewed slowly, simply to have something to do. The rest of the party were scattered around. The only one near Lily was Sir Marsh, sitting a few feet away. He had a ledger on his lap; one she had seen him with before but he currently wasn't writing in it. She was curious about it; what would he write about so much. Glancing over in what felt like the hundredth time, she sighed to herself and rose. A walk in the opposite direction, away from Sir Marsh, might be a good idea. It would be easier to think of something, or someone else, if he wasn't in her direct line of vision. She took several steps forward, intent on not even glancing at him anymore, but couldn't help herself one more time. He wasn't staring out into space like before, instead he was looking at her, clearly bemused. She forgot about her walk as she saw him grin.

'Is there something amusing Sir? Do share, for I love a laugh.'

'Nothing Milady,' Sir Marsh replied chuckling, 'Mostly an inner joke.' When she persisted, he raised his hands upwards as if asking for patience. 'Let's take a walk, shall we?'

Lily agreed and together they moved away from the others. Lily silently waited for him to continue. His demeanour had changed back to thoughtfulness. When they were out of earshot, he half turned to her. 'What do you think about the broken reins?'

'Sir, .. I..'

'Please, Milady, do not insult us both by denying your knowledge of the topic, we both know you were in hearing distance.'

Lily blushed, looking away. 'I must confess I did hear some of it. It is very peculiar that nobody noticed it before.'

Sir Marsh nodded. 'Yes, I thought of that too. I think… no, it's too ridiculous… Forget I mentioned anything.'

'Sir, we both also know I don't just forget something.' Lily smiled at him.

He laughed. 'True Milady, very true. I was just thinking… Many odd things have happened on this trip, I thought maybe someone was trying to sabotage us. It is a ridiculous notion, I don't even know how it came up in my mind. '

'I was thinking the same thing Sir. It is rather peculiar.'

'Yes, it is.' He shrugged his shoulders, 'I can not think of a reason why someone would do that. Why someone would betray us like that. I've never had to deal with a situation like that before.'

'I have.' Lily's voice had changed tone and volume.

'Milady?'

'Betrayal can be many things my Lord, it can seep into the very corners of your own home.'

He scrutinized her, 'I do not think I am certain of what you mean Milady.'

Her gaze fixed on the horizon and the rising sun; she continued in the softest voice he had ever heard her use. 'My mother was murdered when I was three years old. A dagger in her chest. Even now they do not know who the perpetrator was.'

'Do you know?'

She turned to him. Her eyes were glistening with unshed tears, but her face was as firmly set as ever. 'I do not… I was there, and I do remember small things. The song she had been singing to me. The way her hair bounced up and down and the dress she was wearing, but not the person who stabbed her. Nor do I know why. It's all black.' She looked away again. 'All I mean to say Sir is that you need to be careful, even with the people you think you can trust with your life.'

'Even you?'

'How well do you really know me Sir?'

She turned and walked away, leaving him with his thoughts.

Lily walked back to her previous spot, half cursing herself for opening her lips. She had told Sir Marsh something personal, something very few people knew. Her mother's murder was a sore subject for everyone involved. They had never even come close to catching the perpetrator, nor figuring out why her mother had been the target.

Some commotion behind her made her turn around. Two of the soldiers had broken out into argument and were now settling their differences with their fists. Sir Marsh was nowhere in sight, but the Lieutenant was standing only two feet away, staring off in the opposite direction. Why wasn't he doing something to make them stop? This was highly improper behaviour. Lily forced herself to stay; however inappropriate the Lieutenant was being by not doing his duty to control the men, her intervening would be worse. She could do nothing but watch as the two soldiers, who she knew to be brothers, continued fighting.

'Really men, this is unbecoming behaviour.' Mr Johansson almost ran towards the two men. His face showed his anger. 'Stop this right now. Lieutenant, I must insist you stop this.'

Lieutenant Marsh looked at the man as if he had no idea where he had come from. He did not reply. 'Men. Enough, if you have squabbles, you take care of it in your own time.'

The two soldiers ignored him, but when Lieutenant Marsh took his gun and shot into the air; twice, they quickly stopped. Lily jumped. Lieutenant Marsh aimed his smoking gun to them before lowering it. 'I think I told you clearly what is expected of you. Now; GET TO WORK.'

The two brothers quickly saluted and ran away, supporting each other. Nobody said a word after Lieutenant Marsh's outburst. The air was thick with tension. Lieutenant Marsh looked at Mr Johansson and flashed something that was supposed to resemble a grin. 'There, it's over, now we can get back to business.'

Lily could not hear Mr Johansson's response as the two men started to walk in the opposite direction, but she didn't think she was missing anything. Lieutenant Marsh had no trouble using his revolver now, unlike that day when his brother was almost killed. As she rose, she saw Sir Marsh standing a few feet away, partly hidden by a tree. One look at his face told her he had seen everything his brother had done…. And was not happy about it.

He sat down on the rock, angrily punching his fists together. Idiots, all of them were idiots, they were making something that was supposed to be easy, very difficult. And still they were going too slow, despite him trying to put a rush on things. The girl; she was to blame for everything. All that had happened was because of her. If she wasn't so attractive he would blow the whole plan off, but he wanted the girl. She would please him for a while; she seemed like a nice toy.

Not like her maid, he had barely grabbed her wrist before she started to sob so loudly he thought someone would hear for sure. He had let go immediately, apologized, and told her he had been joking. It worked too, so far, the ignorant girl had said nothing to her mistress, but he wasn't taking any chances. It was best to make sure the little maid wouldn't be able to speak at all… and soon.

18
Accident

Eliza was ordinary... no even more than that she was nothing special. She was a servant and nothing more. From her infancy she had been trained by her mother with only one goal in sight; to become the young Miss Lilliane's lady's maid. To honour her family by honouring and obeying her mistress. There was nothing else destined for her.

Nobody cared about her petite figure, her delicate features, or her long golden locks that she took expressive care in to brush every day. Her mind was as well developed as her brother's, perhaps better even, but all that mattered was her status. A servant looks, but does not tell, obeys, but does not question. She was a servant and nothing else was ever expected of her. At first, he had changed that.

She didn't notice it immediately, apart from a fleeting look there hadn't been anything to notice. And when she did catch him looking her way she just assumed he was looking at her mistress. Why would someone like him look at her?

Yet as time passed on she caught him looking at her more and more, even at times when her mistress was not in the vicinity. Could it mean something? Did he see something in her that others, including she herself, did not see? Or was he one of those noblemen that took advantage of young servant-girls. She didn't think he was, but who could tell for sure without evidence?

They had been riding through unknown territory for almost two hours. Her mistress was asleep in the carriage next to her and for once Miss Elliot was silent too. They were passing people; villagers going the same way they were travelling. Some on carts or carriages, others on mules or horses, and many people, old and young, on foot. She had seen them before. Their houses and families destroyed by the war, these people took what they had left and travelled to a new town to settle down. They usually had nothing more than hope of a better life, yet she saw them everywhere in the border-country. Soon they would cross the main river and travel inwards to the capital. She thought they would see less people there.

The road they were taking now was virtually deserted, apart from their party, until they came to a fork in the road. It was hard not to notice her immediately; she looked to be no more than five years old. Her clothes were barely holding together and her hair was long and wild. Everything about her said orphan. She glanced away when the men on the horses came closer and hid behind a tree. Their convoy stopped. Eliza watched as he dismounted his horse and stepped towards the girl.

'Don't be afraid.'

Eliza had opened the door of the carriage on the pretext of letting in some fresh air. She could hear every word he spoke.

'Please Sir,' the girl said, burying her face deeper in her hands. 'I shan't do anything to you. Just leave me.'

'Where are you headed lass?'

The girl made no answer.

'Perhaps you would like a lift from me, my horse is very gentle.' He stretched his hand and smiled at the girl.

Her brown eyes peeked through her fingers at him. Her voice sounded as small as she was. 'I lost me brother somewhere. I was travelling with a cart and horse but I don't know where they are now.' She sniffed, glancing at the others, especially focusing on Eliza and the Misses partly visible from the outside.

'You'll be alright. We won't harm you. You can ride with me and we'll drop you off at the next town over.'

The girl continued to glance at him, unsure of his meaning. Finally she nodded and let him help her up.

The group continued, the girl high up on his horse with him. They rode on in a quick pace. Eliza watched him ride with the girl, who seemed to be relaxing more with every step the horse took. At the next town he helped the girl off his horse, while John helped his sister out of the carriage for a short break. She watched from a distance as he shook the child's hand before turning to her. He smiled at her and she felt herself smile back.

At that moment she did something she would regret later for a very long time for many reasons; she started to trust him.

Lily slowly opened her eyes, blinking as the morning sun fell directly on her face. The curtains of her room were partially opened, just enough for a beam of light to peek through and turn the otherwise dark room, lighter. She was alone in the room; Eliza's cot seemed to have been deserted a while back. The sheets looked cold and forgotten; an imprint of a head had long since left the pillow.

As she rose and dressed herself slowly, she wondered where Eliza could be at such an early hour. Opening the door, Lily went into the hall, checking left and right for her maid. Eliza was not in sight. She lifted her shoulders to herself in afterthought. Where did that girl keep disappearing too?

Lily crept through the shadowed hall of the inn. Her steps echoed in the otherwise quiet building. Here and there a panel creaked from excessive pull by the wind, in the distance a dog howled. Nothing further, no servant shuffling through the shadows, no other presence of a human being but her own; certainly no Eliza.

She was now arriving at a section of the upper floor she had not visited before. One hall led to stairs that went down; probably leading to the foyer, she could tell from the lighting. The other corridor was poorly lit in contrast and seemed to lead to a dead end. Lily was just about to turn around when something small caught her eye. She kneeled to pick it up, studying it carefully. It was a bracelet, made from tiny stones with a smooth outer layer. Worthless to everyone but the owner. Eliza has crafted it when she was five years old. The girl still wore it tucked away under her sleeve, Lily saved hers in her jewellery-box because of equally sentimental reasons. Eliza must have been here. The bracelet could not have been left by anyone else. *When* it was lost however, she could not tell. Their party had been here since late afternoon yesterday. She could not say for sure if her maid still had the bracelet then.

Resolve filled her as she slipped the bracelet into a hidden pocket of her gown. She would look for Eliza throughout this corridor. If someone were to see her, she could always claim to be lost. This inn, though not as large as the last one, had many corridors that seemed to end before they even began. It wasn't hard to imagine getting lost here, just last night she had been headed for the dining room and ended up in the servants-quarters.

A small smile tugged at her lips. That had been embarrassing at the time, especially when Sir Marsh went to open the door for her. He had turned almost redder than she had when they walked in on a maid changing. Eliza had bitten her lip very hard to keep herself from bursting out in laughter. The maid in question had not been as amused, but had, fortunately, calmed down quickly when she realised it was a mistake.

As Lily stepped through the corridor, she kept her eyes open for signs of Eliza, but there was little to suggest that anyone had been here for months or even years. Dust covered the edges of the path on both sides, the few doors there looked to be bolted shut from top to bottom. There was no Eliza, only a dead end ahead. She shook her head, thinking herself very silly for even going two steps in this direction. What reason would Eliza have to come here at all? Turning around, she prepared to go back when a sound from above made her pause. It seemed to be coming from her right. She turned and squinted her eyes to make sure she wasn't dreaming. There was a thin opening in the wall, a niche she hadn't noticed before, barely wide enough to let one person through. The sound was coming from there, a small opening letting in more light as it widened. Laughter flowed down. A voice she knew very well; Eliza. There must be an attic or a balcony of some sort up there, though why, and with who, Eliza was there was a complete mystery. Eliza said something Lily could not hear and another voice answered. She thought it was a man's voice, but nothing about it sparked recognition. The light grew brighter; its sudden intensity as the hatch was removed made her cover her eyes. When they had adjusted, a ladder had been lowered to the floor; Eliza was already placing her foot on a step. Slowly the girl came down, still talking to her companion above them. The sun blocked him from sight; Lily could not even see the colour of his clothes. When Eliza was almost halfway, Lily felt it was time to make her presence known. Whatever Eliza had been doing up there might not be proper and her behaviour reflected on Lily too.

'Eliza.' Lily's voice came out harsher than she meant.

Eliza turned partially, clearly in shock of meeting her mistress here. 'Miss!' she exclaimed, her hand unconsciously going to her mouth.

For a moment the girl seemed to have forgotten she was suspended in midair, her other hand loosened. The ladder toppled forward, while Eliza fell backwards. The girl and the ladder both made a loud noise as they crashed to the ground. Eliza hit her head against the wall, landing on her back and rear. Lily screamed, hastening towards her as soon as the shock wore off. She kneeled. 'Eliza. Eliza? Are you injured? Please say something.'

'Miss…' Eliza looked at her, then looked past her to where the light had been earlier. She tried to speak, but couldn't, her tongue feeling oddly heavy, before unconsciousness took over. Lily shook her lightly, but got no response. She rose quickly. Taking the rim of her dress in her hand, Lily ran the length of the corridor back to their rooms. She spoke softly to Eliza, though it was more for her own benefit then for the unconscious girl, that help was on the way.

19

Apprehension

It was a blur of blackness, mixed with light shining through at unexpected intervals. Voices floated in and out, some she thought she might recognise in a normal situation, but she didn't think she was in a normal anything right now. Her eyes felt heavy, she opened them a slit, checking if the light would do damage. She was lucid enough to know that somehow. The room seemed covered in darkness with the only light coming from something long and thin located at the side. A candle.

'Eliza?'

Her mistress' soft voice broke the last of the fog clouding her mind.

'Yes Miss…'

Speaking was more difficult than she anticipated. Her throat felt dry.

'You've hit your head and have been unconscious for a while. How do you feel?'

'Tired…. My head hurts.'

Lily lifted a cup to her mouth. 'Here, you need to drink a bit.'

Eliza drank slowly. Afterwards she settled back onto the pillow. On the other side of the room she recognised her own cot and realised she was back in their room, lying on her mistress' bed. Her eyes felt too heavy to protest against being treated so kindly.

'I'm so sorry Eliza.'

Even through her haziness she heard the guilt in her voice and wanted to do her best to change it. 'Not your fault Miss. I'm not sure what happened, but it's not your fault,' mumbled Eliza as she dozed off. Lily made sure she was as comfortable as possible. She brushed the hair away from her forehead. If she kept busy, she would think less about how she almost got Eliza killed.

Sir Marsh knocked on the door of the drawing room. He was sure she would be here, there were few rooms left in the inn where she could be otherwise. He had passed by several of them on his way here.

Eliza was doing much better. Cousin Mary was sitting with her now, after he had convinced her Lady Lilliane needed a break. She was blaming herself for the girl's fall, while it was clear to him and everyone else it was an accident. He remembered the look on her face when she came running towards their rooms.

It was a stroke of luck for both of them. He had just come out of his room to go downstairs when she came, almost bumping into him. A few minutes later and they would have missed each other. Her face was flushed and her breathing was ragged, curls were coming out of her bun. Even in a state of panic, he found her the handsomest woman of his acquaintance.

'Oh Sir,' she grabbed his hands as she tried to calm her breathing.

'Milady, what has happened? Are you alright?' her behaviour alarmed him. He knew she was well, but figured something dreadful must have

happened. She was not, unlike his cousin Mary, prone to hysteria and exaggeration.

'Yes, thank you, I am well, but Eliza.... Eliza fell down and hit her head. I think she might be seriously hurt. Please, you must come.'

She turned to run back to where she had come from, with him close on her heels. They had even passed his brother and Mr Johansson, who he had quickly asked to follow them. Together with Mr Johansson, he had lifted the still unconscious Eliza back to her room.

Lady Lilliane had not left her bedside since then. Only now that Eliza was doing better did he convince her to take a walk. He meant for her to go outside, but like often she had a mind of her own.

He knocked again, he didn't want to disturb her, but needed to make sure she was really okay. A soft allowance to enter followed his knock and he quickly opened the door, trying to not look to eager to see her again. He constantly had to remind himself she was meant for their King; he couldn't help but love her whether she was near or not.

When she looked up, her eyes red and traces of tears still on her cheeks, he wanted nothing more but to take her in his arms. Instead he lingered in the doorway.

'I beg your pardon for intruding Milady, I just wanted to make sure you were not in need of anything.'

Lily smiled at him, a soft smile that looked forced surrounded by evidence of earlier crying, a fleeting movement of her lips that did not linger nor echoed in her eyes.

'I'm fine Sir, thank you for enquiring. I'm waiting for my brother.' A chill ran down her back, making her shiver. She rubbed her hands together. 'You may come in if you like.'

Sir Marsh closed the door and took the seat across from her. He hated seeing her so down. Guilt was still eating away at her, if only there was a way for him to distract her. He looked at where she was seated; she had taken a seat behind the writing desk, ink and parchment were out, but she had not written anything yet.

'Am I disturbing you during your letter writing Milady?'

Lily blushed, looking from the supplies she had put out, back to him.

'Oh no Sir, I have put this out for my brother. Donovan is going to write a letter for me. He's going to inform Eliza's parents of her fall.'

He frowned to himself, talking about Eliza or her parents did not qualify as distracting her. He needed to steer her into safer waters.

'Can you not write it yourself? I mean, do you not know her parents as well as your brother does?'

'Yes, I do,' Her smile grew wider, 'Beth, that's her mother, was my nurse. She took care of us whenever my mother, and later my aunt, was not there. She was more of a mother to me than my aunt ever was.' The last sentence was spoken as Lily looked away and drifted into thought. She surprised herself by saying it out loud; her hand flew to her mouth. 'Forgive me Sir, I spoke out of line. My aunt has been very good to me.'

'Do not worry… Lily, she shall not hear it from me. Frankly, she scares me a little.'

Lily laughed at that confession, feeling it bubble up in her abdomen. She couldn't help but feel giddy at her hearing him

The Last Lord's Wife

use her name instead of her title. The informality felt natural. Sir Marsh joined her in laughing.

'There, now you have leverage over me and can be sure I will never tell your aunt what you said. I rather not have her chase after me in a fit of rage.'

Sir Marsh winked at her, a smirk visible on his face. Lily could not help but laugh even more at the image that was forming in her mind; strong, confident Sir Marsh running away from her petite aunt, as she chased him with her fan in her hand.

After the laughter had died down, Lily kept smiling. She was very happy he had come in when he did. She remembered something and decided to tell him the truth.

'To answer your enquiry from earlier,' she began, only slightly hesitant on whether or not to tell him, 'The reason I am not writing the letter myself is because I can not write, not well anyway. I can read, but I was never taught to write properly.' She pondered on how to continue, 'It wasn't thought necessary for a female to learn…. And I agree with them; what use would I have for such a skill.' The last she said in a less than plausible tone.

Sir Marsh, feeling bold, covered her hand with his hand and kept it there.

'Milady, we can learn anything we want. We are not animals.'

'Most men think women are hardly worth more than animals.'

'Most men have not met you,' he rebutted.

She blushed at the compliment, sending him another dazzling smile. He cleared his throat, breaking the moment. He had sworn to himself to help her forget him. Taking her hand was certainly not helping, especially when it took most

133

of his self-control to stop looking at her lips. He longed to taste them again, if only for a moment, to feel her breath warming his cheek, the same way her company warmed him everywhere.

Lifting his hand from hers, he rose and moved his chair backwards.

'Well, if you permit me, I will help you improve your writing skills. How about this afternoon? Business requires me to attend to some things right now, but I am free later.'

'Sir.. I..' she rose too.

He quickly cut off any objections that were coming, 'Milady, it would be an honour. I find writing very pleasurable myself. I have a ledger in which I often write about our travels to keep my mind clear.'

'Very well then. Thank you Sir.'

She curtsied and he offered a low bow in reply.

'You are very welcome Milady.'

He lingered for as long as he dared, before exiting the room. He could feel her eyes burn on his retreating back and wished, yet again, that they had met under better circumstances.

He quickly passed through the inn, going out into the courtyard. He needed air, and lots of it.

It had gone better than he had imagined, he had looked from above as the dumb servant girl fell from the ladder. He couldn't help but smile when she hit her head and lost consciousness. Her mistress was so distressed she didn't even notice him closing the hatch instead of coming down. If he could have been sure he had enough time, he would have finished her off. Her mistress would blame herself and probably not even realise his involvement. It didn't matter; head wounds could turn sour easily, and many did. He quickly climbed off the roof, fixed his clothes and entered the inn, just in time to join another gentlemen heading up the stairs. His luck could not be better.

Lily straightened the parchment again. She had already done it several times but she couldn't help herself. She was apprehensive about her first writing lesson. What if she made a complete fool of herself in front of Sir Marsh? How could she face him again if she did?

She caught herself repositioning the other materials with her mind, rose from the table and left the room. Perhaps Eliza was awake and up for some company. If she was, Lily's presence would no doubt be much appreciated; right now Miss Elliot was keeping watch.

A quick check of the room however, found Eliza asleep and Miss Elliot absent. Libby was drawing something with coal. She quickly rose when Lily entered. Her curtsy was hastened; Lily had obviously caught her off guard.

Eliza was doing well. She had woken briefly, had asked for some water, prior to falling asleep again. Her breathing had evened out to a slow and steady rhythm. The surgeon had high hopes for her complete recovery.

Since it was a possibility Miss Elliot might return soon, Lily felt it best to go back to the drawing room. Meeting Sir Marsh was always better than Mary Elliot. Even if it meant reorganising the material until he came.

When she opened the door to the drawing room, she definitely did not imagine him back already, yet there he was already seated. Had it been a small business affair or had he rushed back, eager to start their lesson? She smiled as he looked at her. The gentle look in his eyes helped her get a tighter grip on her nerves.

Lily closed the door behind her. 'I did not expect you to be back so soon Sir. I hope your business went well,' she said, curtsying as he rose to deliver his own greeting.

'I had an important letter that I wanted to make sure would get sent.'

Sir Marsh retook his place after Lily had seated herself.

'Oh, I am glad.' Lily did not give into her further curiosity by asking more about his activities. She knew if he wanted her to know he would tell her. 'Would you like a beverage Sir?'

Some of her nerves flared up again at the sight of the materials. She tried to distract them both by falling back into routine. After pouring him tea and handing him his cup, Lily sat back nursing her own drink. She found it very odd how she could tell this man she loved him yet be so nervous when he was going to teach her something. Shouldn't bearing all when it comes to her heart be more difficult than this was?

A giggle almost escaped her as she gave that another thought. Before long her nerves had completely faded and she felt almost as eager as he was acting, when they started.

Both took a seat behind the writing table. Sir Marsh took hold of her chair and moved it almost against his. 'It's easier to help you this way,' he said in answer to her gaze.

Lily smiled, but did not reply.

They started with things she already knew. She tried her best to write the letters down neatly and correct. Sir Marsh only adjusted her grip in the beginning. He soon discovered that she was a quick study, something that gave him great pleasure.

As he leaned over her shoulder to direct her pen grip, he kept his breath slow and shallow, not wanting to breathe so close to her face and disturb her in some way. His gaze did not divert from her hand, he felt one more look into her eyes might break the last of his resolve.

They worked mostly in silence. Only his instructions could be heard from time to time. Lily smiled as the lesson continued. She was back to feeling completely at ease with him, he even managed to lessen her guilt about Eliza, just by being near. The capital was the last thing on either mind, their impending arrival there was almost all but forgotten.

20

Surprise

The next morning Lily awoke in a much better mood than the previous day. Her afternoon spent with Sir Marsh had lifted her spirits considerably. She quickly breakfasted downstairs then spend most of the morning reading to Eliza. The maid was doing much better. Her appetite was back and she was in less pain.

Her memory of the event that led to her fall, as well as the fall itself, was lost. There was a chance it would come back but one could ever really be sure with a head injury. Lily could not add more herself. By now she was certain it must have been a male servant of the house, too frightened to come forward, probably worried about his job. She was not sure if it was important. Eliza's behaviour, though not necessarily wise, was without a doubt not improper. Lily could not picture the girl doing anything that could disgrace her.

Finishing the sentence, Lily closed the book. Eliza had sunk deeply into her pillow.

'The book is finished Eliza, what would you like to do now? Would you like me to read something else?'

'No Miss, thank you. You have been too kind to me already Miss. Please, you mustn't worry further about me. I will be fine on my own.'

Lily replaced the book on the shelf. 'I don't mind Eliza. Your health is most important right now.'

Eliza chewed her lips in reflection. 'It's just Miss...' she paused, getting her thoughts into order. 'I am not sure I deserve such attention from you. I've been trying to think of a reason why I would be in that corridor, but I can not think of any. I'm afraid my behaviour may turn out to be disrespectful towards you.' She lowered her chin and dropped her eyes down. 'I am ever so sorry Miss.'

Lily tugged at her hand, lifting the girl's chin with her other. 'I'm sure you could never disappoint me like that Eliza. Try not to think about it anymore. Now, why don't you get some sleep and I'll check in on you again just before noon. Libby will be up soon to watch over you. The sooner you get your strength back, the sooner we can continue, and more importantly, finish our journey.'

Eliza nodded in response, pulling the blanket up to her cheek. Lily waited until she drifted off before getting up from the chair. Libby entered softly; her greeting was almost lost under the volume of Eliza's slumbering.

Lilliane escaped the dim room, exchanging it for the dark corridor instead. She hastened through, not even glancing around her. She had not revisited the corner where Eliza had fallen. Guilt kept from even looking in its direction. Even though Eliza was doing better, and she was as well thanks to Sir Marsh's kind care, she had not forgotten the cause of it all. Her own behaviour; sneaking into a secluded section of the inn; talking so loud it scared another person. She was almost too horrified to even think about. What would her mother have said, if she'd been alive? What would her aunt say if word got around?

She chided herself for letting her thoughts run away with her. They were so far away from the castle, from her home, yet she did not feel homesick at all. Things were definitely done different here, she had adjusted well. Sir Marsh helped her feel at ease simply by being there.

She had never met a man like him; women had their place and fathers and husbands did not care enough to help them become more. She knew not one female who would want more. If there were females that felt they deserved better, it was certainly not discussed. She would be disgraced for the rest of her life, her family would suffer even worse. No, it did not happen in civil society. Yet Sir Marsh was so different, he not only wanted to know her true self, he took pride in encouraging her to grow, even insisted on helping her.

The writing had gone well. Today would be her second lesson. Unlike yesterday, she was not nervous, only eagerness to continue filled her insides.

Lily stopped in front of the drawing room's outer door, raising her hand to knock. She stopped halfway. There were voices inside; someone else was with Sir Marsh, someone whose voice she did not recognise. A female's high twittering laugh followed Sir Marsh's chuckle. Whoever was in there must be an intimate acquaintance. Lily hesitated again. Sir Marsh was expecting her. She could not stay away; it would seem rude. Moreover, if she was honest with herself, she really did not want to stay away to begin with. Curiosity for this newcomer almost overwhelmed her. Knocking softly, she waited for his approval to open the door then went in.

The first thought that came to mind at the sight of their unknown visitor was charisma. Though the elegant female was tiny in stature, she commanded the entire room immediately upon arrival. Her long dark blonde hair was arranged in curls around her face. It added to her natural beauty, but was not ordered in a way that made her look tasteless. Her gown was just as you would expect from a woman of her status and elegance. She was a lady and she was proud of it.

Sir Marsh rose immediately when Lily entered. He offered his arm to her and led her to his guest, who had risen too. 'Lady Lilliane Gaeli of Geastwood castle, I would like you to meet my mother, Lady Catherine Marsh, and my sister, Cathy.' He gestured to the chair next to his mother.

Lily was shocked to find out this woman was Mrs Marsh. She and her son looked nothing alike. If she had seen the lady somewhere else, she would not have guessed her to be Sir Marsh's mother. She was feeling rather overwhelmed with it all; she had not even noticed the little girl before.

The child was young; she looked to be about six or seven. Her blonde hair was the same colour as her brothers' and tied back with brightly coloured ribbons that matched her dress. Cathy's features were a mixture of her two brothers. She had very little of her mother's beauty. Only her eyes were exceptionally bright. A little lighter than her mother's, but much darker when compared to her male relatives. The little girl exposed her missing teeth as she smiled and curtsied along with her mother and Lily.

'I am honoured to meet you Madam.' Lily did her best to keep her voice free from quivering. She turned to the child, sticking out her hand to shake. 'And you too Miss Marsh. You're already quite the young lady, are you not?'

Cathy Marsh giggled and shook Lily's hand. They took seats near each other. Lily kept her lips tightly shut; she was not sure how to start the conversation.

Cathy got up and took the three steps to her brother. 'Can I sit on your lap Willie?' she asked her brother, smiling when he lifted her up.

Lily hid her own smile with her hand. She did not want to make him uncomfortable but found his sister's nickname for him very amusing.

'Well, my dear,' began Mrs Marsh, 'My son tells me you are travelling to the capital.'

'Indeed Madam. My father has entrusted Sir Marsh to guide and protect me on our journey there.' She smiled at him. 'He has been very good to me.'

Sir Marsh's eyes connected with her own. She returned his gaze without constriction until she noticed they were closely monitored by Mrs Marsh. Lily blushed for them both and looked away.

A knock on the door was followed by a servant announcing that their noon meal was ready to be served.

Lily thought of Eliza. 'Forgive me Madam, Sir, I have to make sure my lady's maid gets her food. She has been sleeping.'

Mrs Marsh stood too, her son offered his arm. 'Oh yes, the girl that had the accident. I would like to meet her later, if that is okay with you.'

Lily nodded, 'We would be honoured Madam. Very honoured indeed. Pray, excuse me.' She curtsied and left the room before the others, wondering if Sir Marsh had told his mother everything that had happened on their travels, and whether or not she was happy with it.

She found Eliza awake and sitting up. She was talking amiably with Libby. A tray with food was already positioned on her lap. Lily smiled. Miss Elliot's maid was proving to be more reliable than she gave her credit for. Perhaps she had been too harsh because of her association with Mary Elliot.

The maids greeted her cheerfully; their moods had improved immensely over the last hour. Lily asked about Eliza's health-status and was happy to see she had some colour back in her cheeks. It was decided that Mrs March could visit around dinnertime, if that suited the lady as well. Lily soon left the two to themselves, but not before making Eliza promise to rest again after eating. She did not want the girl to overexcite herself.

The dining room was her next stop. Mrs Marsh, Sir Marsh and the young lady were waiting for her arrival. They also expected Mr Johansson and the Lieutenant to join them. She was most curious to see how John Marsh would be around his mother. Would he act as odd as he did with the rest of them or had she underestimated him like she had done with Libby?

Perhaps there was more to John Marsh than met the eye too.

21
Advice

Lily stepped into the dining room where she knew some of her party to be waiting. She instantly saw they were far from complete. Neither the Lieutenant nor Miss Elliot or Mr Johansson had joined them yet. Mrs Marsh was sitting on the sofa, visiting memories somewhere far away only she could see in her mind. Sir Marsh and his little sister were playing some sort of handclapping game were the six year old kept changing the rules and giggling whenever her brother poked her. Lily smiled at the duo.

Taking a seat next to Mrs Marsh, she tried not to disturb the lady by asking her silly questions or anything like that. They waited in a mutually agreed on silence, only interrupted by the occasional soft squeals of the little girl. Lily was hungry and eager for the rest of the party to come. Nobody was happier than she was when the door finally opened, even though it opened to let Miss Mary Elliot through.

'Oh my dear aunt Marsh.' exclaimed Miss Elliot, holding out her arms to grab the other woman's hands. 'How wonderful it is to see you. You look very well.'

Miss Elliot kissed her aunt's cheek in a whirlwind of ruffles and feathers. Her dress looked exceptionally frizzy today. Lily had to wonder if her dress-designer really enjoyed making gowns like that.

Mrs Marsh's response was more tranquil. 'Good day Mary, I hope you are well.'

'Oh yes indeed, why just the other day, I was telling my dear…'

Mary Elliot proceeded to tell a dozen stories a minute, while Mrs Marsh listened out of politeness and nodded at intervals. Nobody could get a word in between; it seemed Miss Elliot was unstoppable. Though Lily was glad she was free this time, she pitied Mrs Marsh.

Loud footsteps announced the men they were waiting for had finally arrived. Mr Johansson came in first, followed by Lieutenant Marsh and, to Lily's great surprise, Christopher Elliot.

Sir Marsh rose at the sight of his cousin. 'Elliot. When did you get back?'

The two men clasped hands and exchanged pleasantries.

Mr Johansson held his hand out for Mrs Marsh, kissing it when she offered it. 'Madam, I can not tell you what a pleasure it is to meet you at last. I am James Johansson and I am very honoured to serve under your son.'

'Thank you Sir, that is very nice to hear. I am Catherine Marsh, and this is my daughter Cathy.'

Cathy curtsied and smiled broadly. Miss Elliot pulled the child aside and proceeded to talk to her in what she must have thought was the proper tone, but what seemed rather babyish to Lily. It wasn't long till Mrs Marsh put a stop to it, by transferring the child's attentions to her elder brother. John Marsh was still standing near the doorway. He was stiff in his manner and no trace of joy or anything of that sort was visible on his face. He shook his little sister's hand and swiftly kissed her cheek, then proceeded to do the same with his mother.

'Dear John, how are you?' Mrs Marsh caressed his cheek lightly with her hand.

'I am well mother, I trust to find you the same.' At her nod of agreement, he stepped back and rapidly put some distance between him and his mother. Mrs Marsh did not comment, but Lily could see his manner hurt her as her eyes lightly glazed over.

Small talk was engaged, with no input from the Lieutenant's side to continue the conversation. Lily exhaled in relief when noon-meal was served.

She found herself in a pleasant situation during the meal, Sir Marsh was on her left hand and his mother was on her right. Mrs Marsh's nanny and lady's maid, Mrs Thornton, had taken Cathy away to eat in the nursery and afterwards take a nap. The child looked happy to leave her cousin Mary behind.

Miss Elliot was close to sulking during the meal. Mrs Marsh and Sir Marsh were both at the other end of the table. Her brother flanking her right side was the only thing going for her and she had barely said a word since being seated because of it. Lily tried not to smile too obviously.

'And so I don't know who wrote the letter that told me there was an emergency at home, but it was obviously some sort of misguided joke.' Mr Elliot gave a forced laugh, 'I rode home to mother, only to find father was in as good health as ever. I stayed a couple of days to replenish my horse and supplies, before heading back here.' He rose his glass and the others echoed him. 'I'm glad to be back.'

'Here, here.' Lieutenant Marsh emptied his glass in one go.

'I guess we will all drink to that,' mumbled Lily mostly to herself as she sipped her wine.

Her cheeks flustered as she caught Mrs Marsh looking at her, hoping with all her might the lady had not caught on to her meaning. However, if she did, she did not mention anything.

The conversation shifted to travelling and Lily, eager to know more about Mrs Marsh and her reasons for this unexpected visit, decided to strike up a conversation with the lady in question.

'May I be so bold as you ask you something Madam?' Mrs Marsh nodded encouraging. 'I am curious to know, what brings you to this inn, I mean, besides from the obvious reasons of visiting your sons.'

Mrs Marsh smiled. 'Every year around this time, Cathy and I visit my youngest sister, Mrs Mayfield. She lives close to the capital with her two daughters. She is a widow as well. My dear William is always so good to write me letters whenever he's away and when his second-to-last letter came, I was delighted to conclude we were very near each other. We decided to set up this meeting. I am very happy to meet you my dear. My son has told me so much about you. You seem like such a lovely young lady.'

Lily returned the lady's smile. Happiness bubbled up in her stomach and spread through her entire body. All the letters Sir Marsh had written were addressed to his mother, and he was talking about her in them too. She still found it hard to believe at times that such a man loved her. What had she ever done to deserve him? She was nothing more than an ordinary girl, without any worthy accomplishments.

'I am very glad too Madam, it has been a pleasure.'

'Tomorrow, Cathy and I will continue our journey home. You might be interested to hear our house is not far from where you grew up. Only about a quarter mile. In fact, when I was a girl I met your mother once. She and her sister Mariah, that is the youngest one I think, came to a ball my father was holding at our house. I was very delighted with your mother. How is she? I hope she is well.'

At this, Lily swallowed once and bit the inside of her cheek. She inwardly counted to ten to calm herself enough to answer. 'My mother passed away when I was three years old. I was raised by my aunt Louisa; mother's other sister, and my father.' After seeing the look of embarrassment on Mrs's Marsh's face, she quickly added. 'It's alright Madam. You could not have known... How lovely that you met her once. I'm sure she was delighted by you as well.' She smiled; poorly, but the effort was noticeable.

Mrs Marsh, still feeling guilty about stirring up bad memories, expertly changed the subject to a more neutral topic. Grateful for the effort, Lily went along with it. She tried to distract herself, but, like often, her mother was never far from her mind.

She was careful not to let the door fall shut, in case Eliza was asleep and the noise would wake her. The precaution however was unnecessary as her maid was very much awake. Libby was reading to her, but shut the book and rose when she saw Lilliane enter. Lily gestured to the girl that she was excused. Sitting on the edge of the bed, she busied herself by straightening the sheets and blanket.

'How are you feeling Eliza?'

'Much better Miss.'

'Sir Marsh might want to leave tomorrow, if you are up to travelling that is.' She let the question linger in the air.

'Yes Miss, I am.'

Lily scrutinized her to see if she was truthful, but saw nothing that told her otherwise. 'That's good, I am glad... Now,' she rose, 'Mrs Marsh, Sir Marsh's mother, is paying us a visit on her way back home. She has expressed a desire to meet you. Are you up to it?'

Eliza's eyes widened in surprise, she nodded her consent softly. 'Yes Miss.' Eliza lifted herself on her hands. She was curious as to why this woman would want to see her, but Lily had no answers herself. Lily opened the door and beckoned Mrs Marsh to come in.

'Thank you dear, now, would you mind terribly to leave us be for some time.'

'Of course not Madam.'

Confused even more, Lily did what was asked and left to rejoin the others.

Mrs Marsh waited a few minutes before turning to Eliza.

'You must be Eliza, I am Mrs Catherine Marsh, and I have been looking forward to meeting you. I have a question to ask you. Forgive my bluntness.'

'Of course Madam.' Eliza did not have to think twice about her answer. She was a servant and it was what she did. She had never learned to do it differently.

It was up to ten minutes later when Mrs Marsh entered the drawing room where Lily and her eldest son were sitting side-by-side. Lily had taken up her writing tools once again, while Sir Marsh watched her as she put the finishing touches on a letter. She was getting very good at it, something Sir Marsh complimented her on whenever the moment felt right. Lily's cheeks were permanently pink during these lessons. They both rose when Mrs Marsh entered.

'Don't you mind me; I am just going to sit down for a minute. You two continue with what you're doing.' Mrs Marsh sat down on the sofa, taking up needlework that had been disregarded earlier.

Lily and Sir Marsh continued their work, though more reserved than before. Lily found it difficult to concentrate on the task at hand; she was burning with curiosity. Mrs Marsh asking to see Eliza, a servant she had no acquaintance with, was odd enough, but for her to have a private audience with the invalid? She knew though that it was none of her business and she had no intention of prying any further.

Placing her pen down, she lightly moved her chair away from the table. 'I am done with this. Shall we go outside and take a walk? The weather is lovely.'

Sir Marsh echoed her movements. 'I think that is a good idea.'

'Will you join us Madam? And bring Miss Marsh as well?'

Mrs Marsh paused her sewing. 'Yes, I think that is a splendid idea. Shall I invite Cousin Mary along too?' she asked, tongue-in-cheek. The others did not reply. 'You should see your own faces right now,' Mrs Marsh laughed at the pair. 'I think the four of us would be just enough. I shall collect Cathy and meet you outside.'

She stood and left the room, still chuckling over their faces. She thought herself very clever in reading them.

Silence filled the room after her departure. Lily busied herself by cleaning the things she had just used. She pretended not to notice Sir Marsh stare at her.

'Your mother is very kind.'

'Yes, she is. Do you like her?'

'I do, very much in fact.'

Sir Marsh's smile was warm and loving. 'I am glad.' He placed his hand over hers. Lily flinched at the intensity of the feelings that overcame her at his touch. In an instant Sir Marsh took his hand, looking away from her face. 'I apologize. I shouldn't have…'

'Don't,' interrupted Lily, trying to catch his eye again. 'Don't ever apologize for loving me.'

As she spoke the words, he turned back at her and looked her squarely in the eye. His smile grew, but he said nothing, only looked at her. For once she did not look away or blush. What she really wanted to do was kiss him, but thoughts of her father and the capital restrained her. Almost…. She rose on the tips of her toes and quickly kissed him on his cheek. She had never done that before and she could see he was surprised.

'We should go William. Your mother and sister are waiting.'

Lily regretted having to say the words, but she also knew it was needed. They could not stay here indefinitely, though she would not mind if they did.

'Yes, we should go.' Sir Marsh gently caressed her cheek with his hand before turning sideways to offer his arm. Lily took it without hesitation. She only hoped Mrs Marsh would not notice anything about them.

22

Amends

As agreed, Sir Marsh and Lilliane met Cathy and her mother outside. The two ladies were accompanied by Mrs Thornton and her son Peter. They started their walk. At first it was Lily and Sir Marsh in the front, followed by the female Marsh's and, some feet behind them, the two servants, but that changed entirely when Mrs Marsh called her son to her. Sir Marsh excused himself to Lily. She was only alone for a few minutes before Mrs Marsh took the place of her son. Lily peeked over her shoulder and saw Cathy and her brother talking and laughing amiably, the two servants engaged with each other.

Lily turned back to her companion and smiled. 'Lovely day isn't it.' Small talk seemed like the safest choice.

She wasn't sure if Mrs Marsh had a motive for walking next to her, other than simple politeness. The lady seemed to do very little without thinking it through first, a quality Lily thought admirable, but also kept her on her toes.

'Yes, it is.' Mrs Marsh looked at the surrounding land with interest building. 'It is very beautiful here. I am glad we decided to stop. I never really take notice of the land when we are simply passing through.' Lily nodded in agreement. She noticed they had begun to outstretch the others, but was unsure of whether to comment on it. If Mrs Marsh had asked her son to give them some privacy, she must have a genuine reason.

'Your lady's maid is a very lovely girl. I hope you did not mind me having some private time with her. I assure you; I felt it to be needed.'

'Not at all Madam.' Lily did not know what else to reply. Mind it, she did not, but she did still find it odd.

After a few minutes of silence, Mrs Marsh opened her lips again. 'I wonder, have you been away from your home before?'

'No Madam, unless you count a few trips to the river with my mother when I was an infant.'

'I take it you do not have a lot of experience dealing with men.'

Again Lily answered negative. 'Only with the men residing at the castle Madam. And an occasional traveller.' Lily frowned, wondering where she was going with her questions.

'A man in love can stir up a lot of different emotions and expectations, especially when he is as handsome as my son is……. My dear, I know my son very well,' Mrs Marsh replied in answer to Lily's shocked expression. 'The way a man looks at a woman, especially a pretty young thing like you says a lot. He also mentioned you in his letters to me a few times too many for it to be nothing more than a business affair. He's a good man, my William. He would treat you right.' Lily made no reply, 'May I offer you some advice my dear. Old ladies like myself do enjoy sticking their noses in where they do not belong.'

'Oh Madam, you are not old at all,' Lily patted her hand in a friendly way, liking her companion more with every word spoken. 'and any advice you'll give me will be most appreciated.'

Mrs Marsh smiled. 'You're a good girl, I knew that from the moment I saw you.' She took a deep breath and exhaled slowly. 'As females we are instructed to look but not act. We are kept simple. For some of us it is better that way. Take, for instance, my niece Mary. She is the child of my dear sister, and for that fact alone I love her as I should, but wit and intelligence she does not possess. She would be lost in a world where things are actually expected of you, besides marrying well and having children. You and I are different.' Mrs Marsh looked her squarely in the eye. 'We are intelligent enough to do more. I was very lucky with my husband. We married for love you see, though our families were both happy with the connection. Liam, my husband, truly loved me and he encouraged me.' Mrs Marsh smiled as she remembered something. 'He taught me how to ride a horse. It was in our first year of marriage. My father thought it was nonsense for his three daughters to learn such things, but Liam did not agree. He wanted to take rides with me. He even taught me how to handle a sword,' she added winking. 'But don't tell my sons, I don't think they would like the idea very much.'

Lily laughed with her. It was hard picturing the lady with a weapon.

After a short pause Mrs Marsh continued. 'William is more like his father than he cares to admit sometimes. I think that is why they used to butt heads every so often.

John is very different though, he is much more reserved. He is not as straightforward in his manners, still I think that once you get to know him, you'll like him too and I believe, especially with Edmund and my husband gone, it is important to William that whoever he loves has a good relationship with his brother too.' Again she scrutinized Lily. 'Family is important.'

Lily stared back but could not say a word. She knew very well she was hard on Lieutenant Marsh sometimes, but he had done so many odd things. Was his mother mistaken? He could very well be hiding his true self from her; she was not around him that often.

'I understand Madam.'

Mrs Marsh's face relaxed. 'I knew you would my dear.' She glanced over her shoulder where two of her children were with the two servants. 'Shall we continue our walk with the others?'

Lily consented and the lady waved to Sir Marsh and the others to rejoin them.

The conversation turned lighter and more relaxed. Lily could almost imagine this as an outing with family or close acquaintances, if not for Mrs Marsh' words about her sons.

Lily Gaeli made sure she was really alone by scanning around her for other living beings. Seeing none, she slipped her shoes off and lowered her feet in the water. The water was colder than she had expected, the cold created a tingling sensation on every part of her flesh that it touched. She relaxed, laying back on the grass and closed her eyes.

Her mind was so active these days that she had trouble with relaxing. Not only that; she was hardly ever alone for more than five minutes at a time. At home, in the castle, she had spent most of her time with Eliza or unaccompanied. Apart from formal occasions and meals, her aunt let her be. Her father was much too busy. She had her own parlour to do her sewing and occasional drawing, but she was mostly free to do what she wanted. Here it seemed there was someone around every corner. If it wasn't Miss Elliot snooping, it would be one of the soldiers or Mr Johansson.

Lily sighed and opened her eyes. She could hear footsteps coming closer. Someone was already interrupting her private time. She really wasn't in the mood for conversation, whether small or deeply intimate. She lifted herself on her elbows to see who the intruder was. Her determination to stay friendly but also clearly show company was unappreciated, faltered a little when she saw it was Sir Marsh. She couldn't help but smile. He sat down next to her in the grass, still not speaking, and took off his boots. The water moved over her feet an extra time as he submerged his own. Lily laid back down, closing her eyes again. Funny how somehow he knew exactly what she wanted, sometimes even before she did herself.

After the noon meal, a bustle of noise could be heard in the courtyard. Mrs Marsh and her daughter were continuing their journey home and the entire group was seeing them off. Even Eliza had made the trip downstairs clad in several layers of clothing. She was not permitted to stand. The girl had pleaded with her mistress for this privilege. Mrs Marsh had been so kind to her and she wanted to show her gratitude. Lily had consented, though she was not allowed for longer than ten minutes and her brother would accompany her at all times.

Lily had placed herself beside Eliza's chair. She had mixed feelings about the departure of the two females. She had grown very fond of Cathy in the short time she had been with her, Mrs Marsh was very kind too, , but was also a little too observant. Mary Elliot was difficult enough to deal with at times, how did one handle someone kind and perceptive? Lily was not sure there was an answer, yet she really did not need one. Chances were very slim she would ever see either of the ladies again. She was bound for the capital; they were going in the opposite direction, to their home. The capital was not far away now. As soon as Eliza was completely recovered, which should not take more than another day or two, they would depart from the inn as well.

Mrs Marsh conversed with her eldest son and proceeded to say goodbye to him. Cathy was amiably talking with Mr

Elliot. Lily had not yet seen the Lieutenant. When he finally arrived it was only a few minutes till the actual departure. He was rather calm; like usual, neither happiness nor sadness could be discovered in his manners. Mrs Marsh saw him and started to walk away from her son to greet the other.

'Mother, I really wish you would reconsider,' said Sir Marsh, following his mother.

Lt. Marsh grasped Cathy's hand, and quickly patting her head, 'What must she reconsider?'

Sir Marsh addressed his brother. 'I want you to go with Mother and Cathy and accompany them safely home. I do not think it is safe for them to travel with only Peter and Mrs Thornton, but Mother does not want to hear it. She insists they will be fine.'

'Me?' Lt. Marsh sounded surprised. 'Is it not better if I stay with this company? Perhaps Cousin Elliot or Mr Johansson could accompany mother and Cathy. Surely my place is here.' Though Mr Johansson and Mr Elliot were both near enough to hear every word spoken, neither had added anything to the conversation between the brothers. Mrs Marsh was keeping quiet too. Lt. Marsh turned to Mr Johansson. 'Why do you not escort them?'

Sir Marsh answered before Mr Johansson could. 'They are not his family. He has other duties.'

'We really are fine William,' soothed Mrs Marsh, trying to defuse the situation.

Lily could also see he was working up a temper. She wondered if she should, or could, do anything. Nobody said anything in reply to Mrs Marsh. Sir Marsh was glaring at his brother in obvious distain. The Lieutenant seemed oblivious to the situation he had partially created.

Mr Elliot cleared his throat.

'Perhaps I can escort you and Cousin Cathy home, Aunt Marsh. It does not really matter to me whether I travel north or south. Mary is in good hands.'

Mrs Marsh hesitated, but her son had no scruples at all.

'I think that is a splendid idea, Elliot. You know how to honour your family.' Sir Marsh clasped his shoulder and together they walked off.

Lt. Marsh walked off in the opposite direction, sulking. Lily and Eliza, who had watched without commenting, looked at each other but still kept silent. They were no strangers to how odd some family dynamics could be.

When Lt. Marsh walked passed them, he kneeled on the floor and picked up a pillow that had fallen from Eliza's chair, handing it to her with a smile as if nothing had just happened between him and his brother. After catching Lily's look, his face directly went back to blank and he continued on his way.

Lily had no time to think about him further. Sir Marsh and Mr Elliot had returned and they were helping Mrs Marsh into the carriage. Lily rushed forward and quickly curtsied.

'Goodbye Milady, I wish you a safe trip.'

'You too my dear, I hope you end up where you're meant to be.' Mrs Marsh winked at her, before taking a seat inside the carriage.

Cathy waved again. The door closed after Mr Elliot was seated and soon the carriage drove off, picking up speed fast. Lily and the others waved them farewell.

When it was no longer in sight, Lily turned to Eliza and prepared to bring the invalid back inside. John supported his sister back into the inn, with Donovan helping him. Lily would bring the pillows and blanket, while another servant carried the chair. Lily handed everything off to a maid after entering the inn. She kept one pillow in her hand a little longer, studying it.

There was nothing special about the pillow, yet Lt. Marsh had crouched to pick it off the ground. Had it been a random act of kindness or did he do it because the object was associated with Eliza? Had Lt. Marsh been the man with her? If he had been, he had concealed it completely. Not a hint of a prior acquaintance between him and Eliza had come to Lily's notice and, as far as she knew, Eliza had no memory of the event.

Dinner had been awkward and silent all around. Almost everyone present had something to be resentful about. Miss Elliot was constantly sighing and repeating how dreadful it was to say goodbye to ones' friends. She also made it clear she was missing her brother again. Sir Marsh was not speaking much to his brother. Lily had trouble thinking of topics to keep the conversation going; only Mr Johansson was working along.

Lily did not think there was one person not happy to leave the dining room and retire for the night. When she at last crawled into bed and nestled herself under the blankets, she did not think it would take a long time before sleep would come. A single candle illuminated the room. She had been very quiet because Eliza was sleeping and needed her rest. The decision had been made to continue travelling in the morning if Eliza was up to it. Lily hoped she truly was, and would not just say that to please her mistress. Travelling at high speed in a carriage, with a head injury to boot, would be very unpleasant.

Eliza slowly lifted herself on her elbows. 'Is it time to get up Miss? Did I oversleep?'

Lily quickly shook her head, chuckling to herself about the girl's somewhat shocked expression. 'Oh no Eliza, I am actually going to bed. Go back to sleep.' Lily blew out the candle and settled back down.

'Miss?'

'Yes Eliza.'

'I think I am ready to travel again.'

'Eliza….' Lily started.

'I am Miss. I am not saying it because I overheard someone say Sir Marsh wanted to resume travelling. I actually feel well enough to travel again,' her voice grew softer. 'and I've been enough of a burden to everyone.'

Lily sighed, choosing to ignore the last comment all together. She knew she would never be able to convince Eliza that taking care of her had not been a burden. It was a servant's job to take care of her master and mistress and Eliza was a good servant.

'Why don't we both get some sleep and continue this discussion in the morning.'

'Yes Miss. Goodnight Miss.'

Lily echoed the sentiment, turning on her side. Part of her wanted to stay at this inn forever with Sir Marsh, but the rational side of her knew that could not happen. They had to continue and do what was expected of them. She also did not want to continue to socialize with this particular group of people for the rest of her life. She wondered how a group like theirs had ever been constructed to travel together. They were such an odd mixture of personalities. She realised strength lay in numbers, especially in times of war as it was now, but she could not think of another reason such different people would ever choose to be stuck with each other. If it had been her choice, the group would be much smaller than it was now, with a more pleasant atmosphere altogether.

23
Ordeal

With Rose being taken care of by the youngest soldier Robert Pike, and Eliza looked after by her older brother, Lily was free to roam the surrounding countryside. Eliza had been adamant that she was well enough to continue travelling after waking in the morning. And Sir Marsh, after visiting the invalid to conclude his own opinion about her health status, had sided with the girl. Though Lily was not a hundred percent sure it was the wisest decision to make, she did think Eliza was being truthful.

As Eliza's health was no longer a reason to halt their plans, they had organised their affairs and were on their way again before an hour had passed after breakfast.

They had stopped at a cheerful looking field to prepare their next meal and to take a little break. Lily felt the pull of the nearby water tugging at her insides and followed a small path leading her away from the others. The countryside was exquisite, with low bushes grouped together at several spots, and bright yellow wildflowers growing all around.

Lily lifted her skirt up just above the edge of her boots to make it easier to move across the field. The bushes gave way to several high trees, growing close together near the riverbank. Though they blocked the view from the water, they could not hide its unmistakeable sound. A waterfall was now coming into view, blending with the loud noises of water falling. It was much higher than she had expected. It was several feet above her head. She gave herself the pleasure of taking everything in slowly; starting at the bottom and going all the way to the top and back, almost falling from the shock of seeing him there.

Sir Marsh was standing on a rock in the middle of the waterfall at the very top. His chest was bare, he had on pants and, as far as she could see, nothing else. She squinted against the sun, wondering what he was doing up there. He wasn't going to jump, was he? There could be rocks in the water, or shallow ground.

Lily clasped her hand in front of her mouth when he raised his arms above his head. He really was going to jump. She held her breath and stopped herself from letting out anything other than a soft squeal lest she would startle him. Sir Marsh bent his knees before diving off. It seemed like forever till he hit the water; Lily watched his descent in shock. She would never have pegged him to take such an unnecessary risk.

The water had gone almost entirely back to its previous state of semi-calmness before Sir Marsh came up again. Lily released a breath she had not consciously held and, without giving the idea much thought, ran toward the riverbank closest to where he was. Without ceremony she dropped her wrap on the ground and stepped into the water. As fast as the tide would let her, she closed in on Sir Marsh. He had been bathing himself and had only looked up after hearing the splashing she was making. He stared at her in amazement.

'Sir. Are you alright? Did you hurt yourself?' Lily fired her questions without waiting for answers. The water was already coming as high as her elbows.

Sir Marsh broke from his stupor and started to swim. 'Go back Milady, I will come to the shore.'

Lily turned, occasionally looking over her shoulder to make sure he was really coming. She crawled onto the shore, suddenly aware of how she must look. Her dress was soaked and stained with mud. There was a slight rip in the sleeve, where some reed had gotten caught on it and her hair was loose and tangled.

She waited for Sir Marsh to reach the side, offering her hand to help him up. When she had seen to it that he was safely out of the water, she proceeded to check he had not broken anything or injured himself in any way. She could no longer control her anxiety.

'Are you insane? You could have broken something. You could have died. Really Sir, I would have expected better of you.'

To her utmost surprise, and to a certain degree of irritation as well, Sir Marsh started to laugh. He laughed so loud that he could hardly keep himself upright. He leaned with his hands on his knees and continued to laugh. Lily crossed her arms, sending him an irritated look. She had trouble containing her appearance of anger as he continued laughing still. A smile was tugging at the corners of her lips, but she kept firm, biting the inside of her cheek as extra resolve to not give in. Finally, his laughter died down. Sir Marsh arched his back and brushed a hand through his hair as the last chuckles touched his lips. Lily continued to look stern, though she was no longer as mad as before.

'My dear lady. Honestly, there is nothing to worry about. My father and mother often took us to our aunt during my childhood. On the way back, father would stop here and we would swim together. I've lost count on how many times I've jumped off this particular waterfall.'

'Yes, I supposed you're right. It's preposterous to assume that things like nature and rocks in the water change over time.' Lily folded her hands together and contorted her face.

At least Sir Marsh had the decency not to take her last remark as a joke. He checked his remaining laughter, though he did look away for a moment longer than usual.

'I promise you Milady,' he said, taking her hands in his and pressing them together. 'I will not jump off this waterfall again.' He winked at her, 'Or at least not when you can see it.'

Lily grumbled a final time, then let it go, knowing that it was all she would get from him. 'Fair enough Sir. I think they are waiting with the meal for us to return.'

Sir Marsh released her hands and offered his arm. Still dripping with water, they returned to the others.

The reactions the duo got when they arrived back were quite dissimilar for a group of their size. Miss Elliot put her hand over her mouth and, for once made no comment. It was clear from the expression on her face that she was not pleased. When Lily parted from Sir Marsh to quickly change into something dry, she passed Lieutenant Marsh. He too said nothing about her appearance. In fact, he wasn't even looking at her, his eyes were fixed on a nearby mud pool though she wasn't sure he could even see that. It appeared that he, now that his mother left again, was back to his usual self. Lily decided to ignore him and keep on walking.

Eliza looked at her mistress' clothes and was going to get up from her seat to help her, but Lily was faster and pressed her back down gently. Knowing that Eliza would not ask if she did not mention it herself, Lily started a different subject.

'How are you feeling now Eliza?'

'Much better Miss. A little tired from travelling, but I think I can take up my duties again, by tomorrow at the very least.'

Lily shook her head, but did not reply at first. Eliza knew her mistress would be against it, but she also knew she would not stop asking. She was very uncomfortable with so much special care.

'I think a nap would do you some good Eliza, after our meal. I'm not sure when we are going further, but I'm sure you could at least rest for half an hour.'

Eliza knew better than to protest. 'Yes Miss, I think I'll try.'

'Good.' Lily smiled.

She had finished dressing and went to Eliza's chair to help her up. Together they went outside to eat.

Eliza had fallen asleep quickly after laying down. Lily had made Sir Marsh promise to pause for an hour so that the maid could rest properly. He had readily consented.

Lily wandered away from their campsite. She wasn't sure where she was headed, but she definitely was not going back to the waterfall. Sir Marsh might be there again, ready to jump. It was something she did not need to see for a second time

She came to a small clearing and was surprised to see Lieutenant Marsh there. As far as she knew he had been with the others. She hesitated. This was a perfect moment to talk to him and try to get to know him better, as Mrs Marsh had suggested, but she worried about his behaviour. How was she supposed to act if he would act oddly?

She half-turned on her heels when she saw him lift his hand to his eyes. Was he crying? Or perhaps it was just one or two tears. Why he would be upset enough to even get teary was beyond her comprehension. Perhaps he needed somebody who would listen. She wasn't one to probe into other people's affairs, but before she could action her plan of perhaps asking his brother, he lifted his head and looked around.

'Is someone there? I am armed.' His hand went to his pistol.

Lily thought about staying silent and simply sneaking away. If he stayed where he was and not turned her way, she could leave and let them both be, but something in her, something she wasn't quite sure what caused it, did not allow her to move. Perhaps it was born out of her love for his brother, but she had a genuine desire to get to know this odd man better.

Lily gathered her courage and if the conversation turned unpleasant, she could always make an excuse and leave. She kept away from the bushes and walked further into the clearing.

'It's a friendly person Sir. I am no threat to you.'

Lieutenant Marsh turned on his heels. He squinted his eyes in her direction as if he did not recognise her.

'Lady Lilliane?'

Lily did her best to smile. 'Yes Sir. Lovely weather isn't it.'

Lieutenant Marsh looked away from her, to something in the distance. 'Yes, it is.'

Already the conversation was in danger of falling flat. Lily searched her brain for another way to start a conversation, but it proved to be too late, as Lieutenant Marsh prepared to leave.

'If you would excuse me Milady.' He bowed stiffly and turned away.

She let him go on, not knowing a way to talk to this man. She was just about to leave herself when she noticed something oval and small on the ground, near the rock that Lieutenant Marsh had just vacated. Lily picked it up.

'Sir. I think you may have dropped something.' Lily held her hand up in his direction.

The Lieutenant turned back to her, but did not seem to recognise the object. Again he squinted his eyes.

'I am not sure. What is it?'

Lily studied it briefly. 'It's a small portrait.'

The Last Lord's Wife

'Yes.' Lieutenant Marsh walked back to her and held out his hand. 'That is mine, thank you.'

Lily handed it to him. She sat down on the rock. 'You're welcome Sir. It would be a shame if you lost it. One might imagine it to be of strong emotional value, if you carry it around with you.'

To her utmost surprise, Lieutenant Marsh sat down beside her instead of leaving again. She thought she might have been too sentimental for a man like him, but he did not show any type of disgust. Lieutenant Marsh stared in the distance, keeping silent. Lily waited patiently till he was ready to talk. Somehow she could sense he needed some time, but after that he would tell her something important. Something he needed to tell someone.

'Lately, everything seems to be changing. Do you know what I mean, Milady?'

Lily did not, but she consented none the less.

'Some changes are for the better, but one.... one in particular that has been happening to me, is not.' He turned to her directly. 'I am losing my eyesight. Every day I can see a little less.' He looked away again. 'One day soon, I might not be able to see anything at all. I don't know why this is happening. I've been to a surgeon, but he could not find anything wrong with me. He said it cannot be stopped either. It won't be long now before I am blind. I fear that day. It has been constantly on my mind lately. Not being able to see anything, not even this, my most prized possession. I can tell you what it looks like because I have seen it so many times.' He caressed the small portrait with his thumb. 'But the portrait itself, everything very near or too far, has become a blur to me. Sometimes I recognise shapes, but usually only when I am about to crash into them.' He gave a sad chuckle.

Lily smiled in compassion, she was unsure on how to respond. She had never guessed him to be ill in some way. 'May I ?' she asked, he nodded and gave the portrait to her.

Lily held it up in the air; she immediately had to smile at the image. Three little boys stood side by side, their arms around each other. Their little faces were covered with something white, yet not enough to hide their matching grins.

'What is that on their faces?' Lily gestured at the portrait, already forgetting that John Marsh could hardly see her.

'It was Edmund's sixth birthday. Mother had baked a cake with cream on top. We were supposed to wait, but we got a bit excited like young boys can be. The painter father hired made several portraits of us. Father thought it was a good laugh, mother was less impressed. I long for those days, but they are truly gone. Edmund is dead and William… I don't think William likes me that much anymore.'

'Perhaps you should tell your brother about your eyes,' Lily suggested carefully.

'Maybe…. But then I wouldn't be much use to him ever again.'

The Lieutenant looked away from her. Lily thought she saw wetness by his eyes and looked away too, to spare him further embarrassment. She patted his arm with her hand. 'He's your brother. It won't matter to him that you can't be a soldier anymore, I am sure he only wants you to be well.' She smiled at him and though she wasn't sure she could distinguish it, a hint of a smile played on his lips as well.

'Thank you Milady, I guess I should have told someone sooner. It does make feel much better.' He rose, 'I shall look for William now and tell him everything.'

Lily stood too. 'I am glad I could help Sir.'

Out of the corner of her eye she could see someone running towards them. The Lieutenant grabbed her hand and kissed it swiftly, as a token of thanks. Though her feelings towards him had softened with his revelations, she was still glad it was not Sir Marsh who ran towards them. Robert Pike stopped near them and grabbed his sides. His breath came in short gasps, it was obvious he had been in a hurry to get to them.

Lily caught a hint of panic on his face and was immediately alarmed. 'What's the matter?'

'Lieutenant, Milady, you have to come immediately. Sir Marsh found someone sabotaging, he caught him trying to loosen one of the carriage wheels, and now he is holding Sir Marsh at gunpoint.'

'Who is it Robert, who is doing this?'

'Mr Johansson.'

24

Confrontation

The scene that played before her eyes seemed so ridiculous to even consider that she had to blink twice as her mind caught up. Sir Marsh was on his knees, and holding a gun aimed at his head, was none other than Mr Johansson. The look on his face was foreign. She had hardly even seen him frown more than twice in all the time she had been travelling with him; it was too much to even begin to comprehend.

'Mr Johansson? What are you doing?'

Lily couldn't help herself, she had to ask.

He looked at her with his eyes wide, they were red and bloodshed. Was he drunk? Was this some kind of prank? Next to her Lt. Marsh stood stiff as a board, with his hand ready to grab his pistol. He didn't seem to think it was a joke. He looked ready to shoot, ready to kill, Mr Johansson. She realised how dangerous that was. Nobody knew about his eyes. Even if he had the chance, would he be able to hit Mr Johansson?

'Lady Lilliane.' Mr Johansson's voice sounded friendly as always. 'What am I doing indeed? Here I was, minding my own business, only sabotaging the carriage a little bit and dear William had to poke his big nose in.' The words were spoken in a casual way, as if he wasn't speaking about anything worse than the weather.

Lily took a step forward, hesitating when she caught the look on Sir Marsh' face as he flinched.

'Now, now, Milady. I think it's better if you stay right where you are.' He gestured towards John Marsh. 'Same goes for your trigger-happy friend over there. I must say John, I tried my best not to be noticed too much, but with someone like you there, it almost wasn't necessary. I wonder, do you even realise how odd you look sometimes when you're staring off into nothingness. I lost count on how many times I've seen it happen.'

Mr Johansson laughed, but he did not irk Lieutenant Marsh into a reaction other than that he clenched his teeth a little tighter.

'Oh.' Mr Johansson smacked his lips together, 'Seems like nobody wants to play with me, how disappointing.'

'Alright, enough with the childish act. I've heard all the drivel one can bear to hear in a day. Tell me what you want?' Sir Marsh's voice was firm and loud and sounded like it always did. Lily drew strength from his courage. Perhaps he was already thinking about how to get them out of this bizarre situation.

Lily heard a crunch of feet on pebble. She looked up. Mr Johansson's attention was focused on conversing with Sir Marsh. Several feet behind them, two of the soldiers were creeping towards the two men, neither seemed to be armed. In fact, they were dripping water from head to toe and were only dressed in pants and shirts. Lily realised they had been swimming in the river. They did not stand a chance against Mr Johansson, who was armed to the teeth.

Robert Pike was standing behind her, he too was helpless. One soldier was missing. Where was he? Was he in a position to offer them help? She didn't know. What about Eliza. Was her maid still sleeping? And Miss Elliot and her maid Libby? They could be hurt or dead even, and Donovan too.

Her brother. She saw a flash of his tunic in the corner of her eye and willed herself not to look that way; the last thing she wanted to do was put him in danger by blowing his cover.

He was hidden behind a large tree. She had only seen a slight movement of him, but she knew he was there. He probably had the best aim of all if he planned to attack Mr Johansson. She just hoped he was armed.

Something reflected over the field; sunlight had hit something polished. Lily watched the light dance around, hoping, but not sure that this was from the weapon her brother had in his hands. She turned one eye back to Mr Johansson and Sir Marsh. The latter had risen to his feet, the barrel of the gun now aimed at his head. The only good thing about this change of positions was that Mr Johansson's back was now to her brother. She tried not to flinch when several twigs snapped under his feet. The soldiers had disappeared, perhaps taking cover somewhere and regrouping to get weapons.

Suddenly Mr Johansson turned and fired his weapon. Donovan ducked to the ground. He had left the safety of the tree to move closer to them. 'Do you think I'm an idiot boy,' he yelled loudly.

Lily screamed. She started to run but a hand on her arm stopped her. Robert Pike held on firmly. 'Milady, you can get hurt.'

Lily struggled to get him off. The sane part of her mind knew he was right, but all she cared about was Donovan. 'Let me go. He's my brother.'

At that moment she saw two things happen fast out of the corner of her eye; Mr Johansson spun back and hit Sir Marsh across his face with the butt of the gun. He went down for two seconds before getting back up on his knees. He did not seem to be hurt at all. Donovan was dragged to his feet by the, until now, missing fourth soldier, Marcus Peterson. He too was relatively unharmed. The bullet had missed him completely because of his quick thinking. Lily stopped struggling.

'It's about time Peterson.'

The soldier disarmed Donovan and dragged him over to the bulk of the group. 'Sorry Sir,' he replied to Mr Johansson. 'Sit down,' he shouted to the others and forced Donovan down. Lily and Robert followed suit. The Lieutenant remained standing, glaring at Marcus.

Peterson smiled, exposing missing teeth between yellowed ones. 'Sit down *Sir,* unless you want to be shot.'

Sir Marsh called out to his brother, it was a worried man trying to control a situation beyond his control, not a commander speaking to a subordinate, but the message was none-the-less clear. 'John....'

Lt. Marsh complied and sat. The soldier removed his gun.

'You... Sit over there.' Mr Johansson gestured to Sir Marsh and he too joined the others. Now that they had them all together, Lily worried even more about what they were going to do with them.

'Eliza, get up. Get up now.' Lily shook her maid a little rough, but she wasn't really aware of it. Mr Johansson had given her five minutes to collect her maid, Miss Elliot and Libby or he would shoot everyone. Lily was taking him very seriously. The spot where he had hit Sir Marsh had turned from red to purple and her brother had a few scratches from being roughhoused by Peterson as well. She didn't want to put Eliza in danger but she had no choice. Eliza asked no questions, she hurriedly dressed and was putting her boots on when John entered.

Lily rushed to him. 'John. Are you alright? Do you know the situation?'

John's face was grim. 'Yes Miss, I saw. Sir Marsh had asked me to collect some water for the horses and when I came back, he had a pistol pointed at him.' He looked at his sister. 'Where is Eliza going?'

'Mr Johansson ordered me to bring the other females to him. I have no choice but to comply or he will kill everyone.'

'I will go with her.'

'No.' Lily shook her head emphatically. 'He did not ask for you. I think he forgot about you. It's better if you stay behind and try to find the two soldiers, perhaps the three of you can help us.'

'But my sister Miss…'

'I will take care of her as best I can. I'm sorry John, but it's a horrible necessity.'

John admitted defeat by nodding his head. He hugged his sister tightly then quickly left them again.

Lily and Eliza rushed to get Miss Elliot and Libby. Miss Elliot was complying, coming with them without delay. She was quiet and sat next to Lt. Marsh without giving Mr Johansson or Marcus Peterson a second glance. Libby followed her mistress. It was obvious to Lily that they were scared, she shared the feeling.

Lily hesitated a few feet away from the group. Eliza was not moving either. Sir Marsh looked at her and clearly tried to communicate with just a look. Lily understood; she wanted to join them immediately, but could not leave Eliza simply standing there. Mr Johansson was staring at the girl intensely. It scared Eliza so much she was unable to move.

'There are you my beauty. I must say, after all the times I've tried to kill you, you still manage to bounce back with all your loveliness intact.' Eliza's face turned from fear to shock. She frowned. 'Yes. I know you do not remember anything. On the one hand, it is a shame because I did enjoy some of our time spent together, on the other hand, it's nice to know you don't remember. Those who do not recall can not rat you out either… You will be glad to know Milady,' he turned to look at Lily, '….. that your servant never said anything about you. I wanted to see if she, by way of you, knew anything about Sir Marsh's plans, but if she does, she never even dropped a hint. It was why she was no longer of use to me. Since her little fall from the ladder did not do the trick, I thought a tragic accident with the carriage might work. Unfortunately that's when I was caught. We would have nearly made it to the capital too.'

Sir Marsh almost yelled. 'Why did you do it Johansson? Why did you sabotage us? I mean, cutting the reins in half, my stable-strap so I would fall, setting the stables ablaze… Why go through all that trouble?'

Mr Johansson shrugged. 'I guess because I had the opportunity, and it was fun.' For a moment he seemed to be drifting away with his thoughts. When he spoke again, his voice was almost a whisper. 'And because she wanted it. I have to do what she says. I owe her that.' He continued in a normal volume, 'Although, I must say when the Elliots were added to our group I mostly focused on getting rid of some of the travellers. Such a large group travels too slowly.' He smiled. 'At least I got rid of one of the Elliots.'

Lily took the opportunity to grab Eliza's arm and drag her over to the group. Mr Johansson followed them with his eyes, but did not comment. Lily pushed Eliza down next to Robert Pike and sat in front of her. She had promised John she would take care of Eliza and would do her best even if it meant getting hurt herself.

Mary Elliot stared with wide-open eyes at Mr Johansson. 'What do you mean by that? What did you do to my brother?'

'So you really want to know everything I did?' Mr Johansson laughed. 'Getting rid of Elliot was easy. Although not as fun as killing him would have been, I bet he would have squealed like a pig. I simply wrote him a letter to lure him away. You really should have gone with him Mary, it would have saved you from the fate you are destined for now. I gave it to our favourite Lieutenant and simply told him a courier gave it to me. There had even been a real courier that delivered a letter for Donovan. I couldn't have planned it better myself.' He rubbed the pistol with his free hand.

More alarm-bells went off in Lily's head. She thought of John and the two hidden soldiers. They needed time to help them. Stalling. That was the best technique right now. Keep Mr Johansson talking until they could be rescued... if they were rescued. Lily felt fear course through her entire body. It wanted to clench her throat shut and took over her heart rate. Sir Marsh reached out next to her and briefly brushed her hand. She wished he could hold her tight and whisk them all away to some place far. It was surreal to have a man they had trusted enough to travel with, turn on them in this way.

'What about the night wandering?' Lily managed to speak without quivering. She was proud of herself and even straightened her back a little more. She would not give him the satisfaction of seeing her afraid.

'Sometimes that was me, sometimes that was Peterson here. It's easier to do things at night.'

Mr Johansson looked around him, suddenly nervous. 'Peterson, why don't you tie them up. Start with the men and then do the women. We'll figure out how to deal with them later.'

The soldier nodded, and left to get some ropes. He was out of sight for two minutes when a sudden explosion made everyone jump where they were seated. Mr Johansson spun around fast, but then quickly turned around again when he realised his back was now towards his prisoners. 'Peterson. Come here.'

The soldier quickly returned. He had only grabbed one rope before returning with haste. 'Yes Sir.'

'Go. Find out what that was.'

Peterson looked frightened and did not move. 'Sir…I…'

Mr Johansson swore under his breath. 'Fine. I will go. Here.' He shoved Lieutenant Marsh's confiscated weapon to him and raced off to where the explosion had occurred.

Sir Marsh nudged his brother as soon as Mr Johansson was out of sight. Lieutenant Marsh grabbed a handful of pebbles in his hand, and when Marcus Peterson's attention was focused on something else, threw the pebbles as far right as he could. The already uneasy Peterson spun on his heels. Sir Marsh was up in a heartbeat and tackled him. They fought over the gun, but even though Peterson was a highly trained soldier, he was no match for the much stronger William Marsh. The traitorous soldier was on his back, his hands tied together with the one rope he did manage to collect. Sir Marsh gave the gun back to his brother and armed himself with the soldier's pistol. He glanced at Lily and the others, gesturing with his hand for them to get up, but to keep as silent as possible. They grouped together.

'Milady, Miss Elliot, please take your maids and hide in the woods. There is a cave at the waterfall, it's safe in there. We will come for you as soon as we've apprehended Johansson. Donovan, go with them and protect them as best you can.'

Donovan nodded.

Lily wanted to say something, but did not know what. She locked eyes with Sir Marsh and managed to produce a weak smile. They were still in danger, the men more so even than the females, since they were staying behind to try and capture Mr Johansson. One of them, or both, could be killed. Sir Marsh nodded to her, doing his best to reassure her. Mary Elliot and Libby were already halfway to the trees. Eliza and Lily made to follow when another loud noise stopped them dead. Another bullet had been fired. Johansson was back.

'Peterson, you imbecile. I can't even trust you with such simple task as this.' Mr Johansson quickly moved forward, his gun at the ready. 'Where is everybody going, we were having so much fun. I wasn't really aiming at anyone just now, but I can easily change that.'

Sir Marsh lifted himself to his full height. It was an impressive sight, one that the medium sized Johansson could not compete against. Lily was only a few feet behind Sir Marsh, still very close to Mr Johansson. Eliza was behind her. The two other ladies had made it safely towards the trees and were now observing everything, while protected by large trunks.

'It's over Johansson, we have your lackey and you have nobody else left. It's just you against all of us.'

'Perhaps, but you forget Marsh, I have the gun. You're right about one thing though, I am getting tired of this. I think it's time to put an end to all this nonsense.' Mr Johansson glared at Lily, 'Starting with you. Goodbye, Lady Lilliane.' He spat out the last words as he aimed his pistol directly at her.

Lily was frozen, unable to move her body. Mr Johansson pulled the trigger, the bullet sailed through the air. A bloodcurdling scream confirmed it had hit a target, but not the intended one. Lily was lying on the ground, relatively unharmed, looking at the person who had pushed her aside. Someone was hurt, in a life threatening way. Another shot sounded, before nothing but silence followed.

25

Conclusion

'Donovan.' Lily's voice was shrill and high from the shock of seeing her little brother get shot. She quickly crawled to him and cradled him in her arms. He had been shot point-blank in the chest and was losing blood rapidly. Lily started to sob even as she was pressing a rag against the wound. Donovan coughed, blood coming through his mouth.

'Are you.... okay.... Lily?' he managed to stammer.

Lily nodded. 'Yes. Why did you do that? Why did you push me away?' She wiped a trickle of blood away from his face.

'Couldn't let you get hurt. I'll be okay Lil.'

Sir Marsh kneeled beside them on the other side. His gaze met Lily's briefly, but she quickly looked back to her brother. She couldn't take what she read in his eyes.

'Yes, you will be.' Lily answered Donovan softly. She wiped the tears away and brushed through his hair.

'You did good lad.' Sir Marsh's voice was choked by grief. 'I'm proud of you.'

Donovan faintly smiled. 'Thank you Sir. Take care of my sister, please.' At Sir Marsh' nod, he glanced back at his sister again. 'Lily, it doesn't hurt anymore.' He barely had the energy to finish his sentence before his eyes rolled to the back of his head. He coughed one last time, before all was silent.

Sir Marsh stood, shouting orders to everyone before half running in the opposite direction. Lily felt blank, hollow inside. She carefully closed her brother's eyes, then cradled him tighter to her and wept.

James Johansson was dead. His last shot had entered his own chest, killing him instantly with hardly any pain. Lily didn't think it was fair. He should have suffered longer, like her brother had. The man who had been responsible for so much of their suffering had taken the easy way out.

Lily stared ahead, not seeing anything. Her grief had been buried now that Donovan was no longer in her direct vicinity. She felt empty and drained. All she could think about was her brother and how unreal it all seemed. As if it had been nothing but a nightmare and she would wake up soon to the sounds of her brother's laughter.

'Miss?' Eliza stood behind her, holding clean cloths and some basic nutrition. 'Miss? I really think you should eat and rest. Or at least rest.'

Lily shook her head slowly. She wanted nothing. Her dress was caked with dried blood, dirt and grass stains, she didn't even have the energy to wash up and change.

Someone placed a soft hand on her shoulder. Sir Marsh leaned in close to her ear. He smelled of moist earth mixed with sweat. 'Miss Lily, please. You'll feel better once you've cleaned up. Let Eliza help you. After that you can sleep as long as you like.'

This time Lily nodded yes and even began to get up. The pressure of Sir Marsh's warm hand did what Eliza's soft coaxing had been unable to do. She allowed Eliza to help her change, and after being refreshed and consuming some of the water and food, she was put to bed.

Sir Marsh's hand caressing her cheek softly was the last thing she registered in her mind before she fell asleep.

The funeral was that evening. Sir Marsh had dug the hole himself, on a small hill that overlooked the forest on one side and led to the water on the other. Lily clutched to Eliza's arm. Eliza was leaning on her mistress too; they needed each other to stay upright. Sir Marsh led them in prayer. The three remaining soldiers covered the grave with dirt.

Robert Pike had constructed a simple wooden cross and spent the afternoon carving the name of the deceased in it with his knife. He died a hero he had told Lily when she saw it, and deserved all the respect they could give him.

Sir Marsh had spent most of his afternoon sitting in front of the tent Lily was sleeping in. Nobody spoke to him. Only Eliza brought him food and wine at regular intervals.

John and Lt. Marsh had taken the prisoner to the nearest army base. Marcus Peterson had denied knowing about the female Mr Johansson had mentioned or his other motives. He had only gone along with him because he had been offered more gold than his wages and the maid Libby to use for his pleasure. Mr Johansson body had been burned by the soldiers.

It was a dead end, literally. The survivor knew nothing; the deceased had taken his secrets with him to the grave.

After the funeral, they went back to their camp and packed up. Though it was already approaching dusk, nobody wanted to stay there. It wasn't safe to travel in the dark but luckily the army base had turned out to be only a few miles away. Sir Marsh helped Lily into the carriage. Donovan's horse had been tied at the back. The two other horses were sold to the army. There was no need for them anymore.

The other females joined Lily in the carriage. Miss Elliot sent Lily a sympathising look. The lady had hardly uttered more than ten words the entire afternoon. They had all been silent.

Sir Marsh tied Rose to his stallion. He signalled to John to start the carriage and gave Andiamo a nudge. They were off again, minus three of their fellow travellers.

Lily carefully pulled the comb down. Her dark hair was still wet from the bath she had finished ten minutes before. Soon it would be dry again and her curls would return. She only had a few at the end, Frederick had much more, like their father. Donovan's hair had been entirely straight; he had loved her curls.

As a young child, he often hid his face in them. She would carry him around in the corridors of the castle. He had been two and she was almost six. Little Freddy didn't like to be held, he preferred to sit on his rocking horse or running as fast as his chubby little legs could carry him. She had missed the constant companionship of Frederick since leaving home, but Donovan had filled that void. Now Donovan was gone forever and she wasn't sure she would ever see Frederick again. It was a cruel and constant ache in her chest. Something she did not think anything could ever take away.

Only Eliza and Sir Marsh had managed to brighten things for her these last few days. Eliza had proven to be irreplaceable in every way. It was almost as if the girl had developed a sixth sense to all her needs, often before she knew she needed it. Lily was sure she could not have survived without Eliza.

Sir Marsh's support had been different but equally wonderful. They had taken long walks together, sometimes not speaking at all, sometimes filling every minute with memories from both their childhoods, as well as horseback-rides whenever she needed to let off some steam. She had even cried on his shoulder once after suddenly coming across something that had belonged to Donovan. They had grown even closer than she could have imagined.

The one good thing that came from all of this, she knew it had grown after she lost her brother, was that she was now absolutely sure that she did not want to let William Roderick

Marsh go, ever. Somehow, someway, she would find a way to please her father and still fulfil her heart's deepest desire. A hint of a smile appeared on her lips as she put the finishing touches on her hair and hopped into bed.

A loud thunderclap echoed through the nearly clear, grey sky, signalling the arrival of the long expected thunderstorm. Lily rose from her seat and settled herself on the windowsill; she drew the curtains back with her hand. The day had been uneventful and mostly silent.

Sir Marsh and the soldiers had been checking all their equipment for possible sabotage. John and the Lieutenant had taken the carriage and all the horses away with a similar goal. Sir Marsh was taking no chances. He was determined to not let Mr Johansson taunt them from the grave. Eliza and Libby had been cleaning and washing all day. Miss Elliot was taking a nap. Lily was alone and rapidly becoming very bored. Sir Marsh had practically ordered her to take it easy, but without anyone else around it was becoming very tedious indeed. It was ironic; she could almost laugh about it; when you wanted to be alone, there were people everywhere and now that she wanted companionship...... She sighed. It was going to be a long day.

More thunder exploded through the air, followed by a sudden summer shower. Lily released the curtains. She picked up her skirts, running through the halls of the inn and outside through the front door. For once, she didn't care who was able to see her. Stretching out her hands towards the sky, she circled around, letting the rain completely soak her. Lily started to laugh. The rain tickled her face and arms and mud was pooling around her shoes. For the first time since Donovan's death Lily felt she could some day be happy again.

The sound of hooves on stone was getting louder. Lily stopped twirling, gazing into the distance. The men only nodded their heads quickly before leaving. Some went into the barn to dry the horses off, others went into the inn to put their things away.

Sir Marsh stopped and looked at her with a mixture of surprise and bemusement. 'Milady, should you not return inside? You'll catch your death this way.'

Lily grinned in a way that made him slightly uneasy. They were completely alone by now, with only the continuing pouring rain as a companion. The thunder had stopped.

'I will soon… but not before doing this.'

Lily threw a handful of mud towards him. Sir Marsh was caught unaware and most of the mud hit him squarely in the face. He rubbed it off with his hand then looked at Lily. She was laughing quietly, her entire body shaking with mirth.

'Looks like you are a little dirty William,' she added with a taunting undertone.

Sir Marsh kneeled and scooped his large hands full with mud. 'Miss Lily…. You are going to pay.'

He started to run towards her, but Lily was ready for him and quickly ran in the opposite direction. A full-out mud war was on, with the participants chasing and hitting each other with mud without actually touching. Their laughter was almost as loud as the rain falling down.

When they eventually walked back into the house, both were covered by mud where the rain had not washed it off. Lily was still giggling at intervals and Sir Marsh was clearly amused too. They separated at the top of the stairs, Sir Marsh winked at her before turning left, making Lily giggle again. She turned right towards her own room, trying her best not to track mud and raindrops all over the floor.

Her room was empty, Eliza was absent. Lily stood in front of a full-length mirror and inspected her clothing. If her aunt could see her now; she would definitely be horrified, but Lily, for once, did not care. If Donovan had been here, he would have joined them. That thought alone had made her throw more mud.

Lily carefully removed her dress and placed it aside. When Eliza came, bathwater was collected. And even when it proved tricky to remove the mud from her hair and skin, Lily remained in good spirits for the rest of the day.

The storm continued through most of the night. By breakfast however, the sun was already so high up in the sky that all evidence of rain had dried up.

Lily consulted Sir Marsh about their affairs and was not surprised when he told her they were leaving again after breakfast. The capital was very near now; their journey was soon coming to an end. Their arrival in the capital meant several changes for them all; Mary Elliot and Libby would leave the group. A manservant would accompany them the remaining ten miles to Miss Elliot's intimate acquaintance. She was expecting them.

Lily would not go further, her ultimate destination was the King's castle, but first she was to go to the convent. Sir Marsh would escort her. There they would wait until the King could receive them.

Lily was silent as they prepared their horses for departure. Next to her, Sir Marsh worked in a quick tempo, glancing at her at regular intervals. He smiled whenever she happened to catch his look. A small tugging at his lips conveyed all his current emotions to her. He was easy to read now that she had gotten to know him so well. That she felt the same at the moment helped understanding him even better. She was anxious about the capital and worried that the King would choose her as his wife.

With Rose ready, she mounted and waited till the signal for departure was given. Lieutenant Marsh had made an excuse to ride next to John on the carriage. With all that had happened lately she had forgotten about his eyes. She wondered if he had told his brother the truth yet, but did not think he had.

Sir Marsh shouted a last order to the soldiers, before they were all off. She rode next to him at a steady pace, only answering when he asked a question. Her mind was elsewhere, but she knew he did not mind.

They stopped for their noon-meal at a clearing where a handful of houses had been built and bought freshly baked bread and ripe fruit at a small market. The berries stained their hands and turned their tongues blue. Lily laughed at her reflection, she put some fruit aside for later and also bought some herbs to restock her medicine pouch.

They rested on top of stones, next to the horses, listening as Robert Pike sang songs native to his village. When everyone was refreshed, they continued their journey in the same pace they had ridden in before. This time Lily rode in the carriage with Eliza, Miss Elliot and Libby. She soon fell asleep to the constant chattering of the lady. When she awoke, it was near dusk and they had arrived in the capital at last.

26
Arrival

As the carriage pulled to a stop at a small inn that was the destination for two of their travellers, Lily did her best to seem calm and composed as always. She could not help but feel glee at the thought of saying goodbye to Miss Elliot. No more endless chattering, no more remarks that were slightly inappropriate but still said in a pleasant tone. The level of general conversation would surely be improved.

Sir Marsh opened the carriage door and extended his hand to his cousin, but Miss Elliot's mind seemed to be far away. She did not reach for his hand, nor did she put much care into placing her feet properly. Her left foot missed the step completely and floated on air instead. Miss Elliot plummeted forward. Lily covered her mouth in shock, reaching out with her hand to try and grab her, but it was too late. Miss Elliot fell off the carriage's steps with a loud scream. Sir Marsh quickly jumped forward, grabbing her by the arms and keeping her from landing flat on her face. Miss Elliot stumbled a little.

'Oh Sir Marsh,' she exclaimed, 'Thank you Sir. I might have broken something if you had not helped me. Did you see how brave he was Lady Lilliane? I could have been severely injured.'

Humouring her, Lily stepped down herself and took her arm, leading her away from the carriage. 'It is very fortunate indeed. I think it's best if we get you checked out though, just to be sure.'

Lily decided to show her the respect she had not earned, and slowly led her away from the place that had been her public humiliation. Sir Marsh chuckled one last time before continuing on his way.

Lily placed her arms on the railing and breathed in the soft evening air. The sun had nearly set behind the mountains that seemed so far away still, and a soft rain earlier on in the evening added a warm melancholy feeling to the air. The veranda Lily stood on was partially shadowed in darkness; to Lily it felt too much like her life right now. Her past was behind her; there was no going back to her sheltered upbringing and she had trouble imagining any light in the future either. Especially since it held neither her brother nor the man she loved so dearly.

Sir Marsh came around the corner of the house and stopped next to her. He echoed her pose by placing his own arms on the veranda railing. He breathed in deeply and closed his eyes. Lily smiled softly.

'It's hard to believe that we are actually done with travelling. As a group I mean, I will be travelling home soon.'

Her muscles tensed. Knowing that he would be leaving and hearing him say it were two different things she realised.

'I know Sir,' she managed to reply to his inquisitive stare.

He placed his hand over hers, still present on the railing. 'I wished it would have gone different.'

Lily agreed with him, she could say nothing else but repeat her earlier statement. 'I know Sir.'

He squeezed her hand; he understood.

They froze in place, enjoying each other's company in a way they both knew would never happen again, Lily hardly dared to breathe. She wanted nothing to disturb this moment, only when footsteps in the distant were obviously getting louder did they move apart.

'Brother,' Lt. Marsh hesitated some feet away. 'Can I have a moment with you, alone?'

'Can it not wait?' Sir Marsh sounded annoyed.

Lily guessed, as she saw how nervous Lieutenant Marsh seemed, that it was probably about his eyes. She carefully placed her hand on Sir Marsh's and softly whispered to him. 'I think it's important.'

Sir Marsh looked back at her, surprised at her intimate gesture even though they were not alone. He did not know his brother could hardly see them. He nodded and giving her hand one final squeeze, he followed his brother and left her alone.

Lily turned back to the setting sun. It was good that the Lieutenant was telling his brother about his eyes. She imagined it was a difficult thing to talk about. The view no longer seemed interesting. She smiled, leaving as well. Perhaps Eliza could distract her from what seemed like an unavoidable doom.

'Excuse me Milady, may I be so bold as to interrupt you?'

Lily looked up from the book she had been reading for the past hour or so and scrutinized the individual that had spoken. He was a stranger; someone she had never before laid eyes on. His dress was not peculiar for this region; she could instantly tell he was not an outsider here as she was. At least he seemed pleasant enough if she went by the measure of his smile.

Quickly she rose, dropping the book on the chair she left behind.

'How can I help you Sir?' Lily was intrigued with this new arrival; it was rare to meet someone so suddenly and in such an odd way.

The gentleman twirled his hat around in his hands. 'I beg your humblest apologies. My name is Thomas McKenzie; I am looking for Miss Mary Elliot. I am to escort her to my sister's lodgings. A servant let me in through the door, but I'm afraid the poor chap fell ill suddenly, and could not escort me any further.' He gave a half smile. 'This house is build like a maze.'

'Please sir, why don't you sit for a moment?' He gladly accepted. Lily poured him some tea and then proceeded to ring a servant. 'Please tell Miss Elliot she has a visitor.'

The servant nodded and left again. Lily retook her seat across from Mr McKenzie. She offered him more tea and poured them both another cup. It was difficult to decide what to do in this situation. She knew not what she could strike up an exchange about. Finally she decided to talk about the one thing she knew they had in common; Mary Elliot.

Without trying to pry in Miss Elliot's affairs, Lily started a conversation. 'Have you known Miss Elliot long?'

Mr Mackenzie took a sip from his tea. 'On and off. My sister is a dear friend of hers. She regularly comes for a visit at our mother's house, though this year it is somewhat earlier in the season. I understand she felt obligated to travel with her cousin.' He chuckled at this, and leaned back in his chair. 'Though I do not doubt it was agreed upon with mutual pleasure, I heard her cousin is quite found of her.'

The last was said in a mock-whisper, followed with a wink. Lily did her best to make her smile seem genuine. Clearly Mary Elliot's acquaintances knew very little of her actual life apart from what the lady told them herself. Lily conveniently changed the subject to a more general topic.

A full ten minutes passed and still Mary Elliot did not appear. The servant had reported not being able to convey the message; as he had been unable to find the lady. Mr McKenzie was indeed a pleasant conservationist, yet Lily found herself being less open than she would normally be. Mr Johansson, she remembered well, had been very pleasant in his manners too. She felt weary of travelling and meeting new people. Perhaps there was something to be said about reaching one's destination after all.

A silence fell that enfolded the entire room in pleasantness, until the door was suddenly opened accompanied by a lot of noise.

Sir Marsh entered, looking over his shoulder as he yelled something at his brother. 'And you can tell him he had better have his gear in order before I get back outside again or I will break both his legs.'

Lily blushed for him. It was not a good first impression to make on someone.

Sir Marsh turned around. His expression changed to one of surprise, as he looked from Lily to the stranger. 'Sir William Roderick Marsh. How do you do Sir.' He clicked his heels together and his body position stiffened.

McKenzie rose and they both bowed a ceremonial greeting. 'Thomas McKenzie. I am to escort Miss Elliot to my sister's house. Lady Lilliane was kind enough to entertain me while a servant fetches her.'

McKenzie winked at Lily who smiled back out of politeness. Sir Marsh however did not look pleased. He quickly pushed a chair next to Lily and seated himself. McKenzie sat down in the same chair he had occupied earlier. Lily prayed neither of the men would embarrass themselves further, but her worry seemed unfounded. The gentlemen easily glided into a conversation as if they did nothing else but converse with each other. Lily found her mind wandering away from the conversation. She wondered what was keeping Miss Elliot. The lady was pushing the boundaries of proper society and without a clear reason.

Miss Elliot's entrée was contrary to everything Lily had witnessed before; one of poise and propriety. If she had not looked up at the door at that very moment, she might not even have noticed at all. For the soft tapping of Miss Elliot's shoes were nothing compared to the thunderous voices of the two men loudly discussing something political and uninteresting to ladies. She quickly curtsied to the men, hardly giving them time to perform their parts before she sat down. Lily offered tea, but she declined. The men suddenly felt uncomfortable and since it seemed that Miss Elliot was not going to be a good hostess, they continued the conversation they were having before her entrance.

Miss Elliot was gone, whisked away by her acquaintance's brother only an hour before. With her the only thing keeping them together. The last few miles vanished under her as the carriage drove her quickly to what would become Lily's new home. The weather fit her gloomy state of mind; it had not stopped raining since they left the inn. On the contrary, the wind was doing its best to compete with the drops on who was the loudest. It made Lily uncomfortable; for herself and Eliza, but mostly for their companions riding their horses and doing their best to guide the carriage safely through the storm.

Next to her, Eliza shivered, she couldn't tell if it was from cold or anxiety. Lily turned to adjust the blanket her maid had around her. The carriage suddenly stopped, Lily fell forward, unable to keep the little balance she had. Eliza's blanket cushioned the blow of the fall. She tried to get up with some dignity; Eliza's hand was a big help with that.

'Thank you Eliza.'

'Are you injured Miss?'

Her reply went unheard as the door opened. A soldier appeared, the rain dripping down his coat and face.

'Everyone alright?'

'Yes, Mr Fletcher. May I ask what's going on?'

Fletcher raised his voice to be heard over the howling of the wind.

'Unfortunately, a wheel is stuck in a pothole. We are attempting to fix it now. Hold on.' Lily nodded and sat back on the seat. Next to her Eliza shivered from the extra cold that had entered through the opened door. The soldier had left them again.

Lily waited, several minutes went by and she grew impatient. Eliza had fallen asleep; a blessing for the girl who was still unwell in many ways. Lily grabbed her wrap, draping it around her shoulders. She had made a decision and was not planning to stray from it. Opening the door, she climbed out of the carriage. She made sure to close it properly, Eliza had to stay warm.

The men were working at the back. John was in front; ready to pull the horses forward, while the three soldiers and Sir Marsh were doing their best to get the wheel out of the pothole.

The Lieutenant was holding the remaining horses tightly by their reins. It was unfortunate that there were no trees around to tie the animals down, the lightning and rain did not help.

Lily lifted her skirt up to her ankles, dropping down in the pothole next to Sir Marsh. The soldiers looked up in surprise, but did not say a word. The grins on their faces were unmistakeable. Robert Pike bit his lips.

Sir Marsh scowled. 'You're going to catch your death out here.'

'So will you.' replied Lily, mimicking his movements by pulling at the wheel.

Sir Marsh's nose wrinkled, though he could hardly hide his grin. He knew it was useless to argue further. Moreover, if he was honest, he was soaked thoroughly. Any help to get to shelter sooner was welcome, even if it came from a woman.

As the soldiers shovelled sand away, Lily and Sir Marsh replaced it with straw and twigs. It was nearly another half hour before the wheel was secure enough to try to move forward. The wheel turned on the straw, at first it appeared still stuck, but after John had whipped the horses a second time their added strength brought some movement to the carriage. Robert Pike joined John with leading the horses and the carriage finally broke free.

Sir Marsh climbed out of the pothole and offered his hand to Lily. She accepted it gracefully. 'Milady please, get back into the carriage before you catch cold.'

Lily smiled and decided not to argue. 'Yes Sir.'

She turned; however, Sir Marsh had not released her hand. She turned back, a question in her eye.

'And, thank you,' he said.

'You're welcome.' Her hand was released. Lily climbed into the carriage. Her dress was soaked with rain and there were stains of mud. Even as she shivered, she could not hide the red blush on her cheeks.

Sir Marsh ordered the soldiers to fill the pothole with as much straw, twigs, and mud they could find, lessening the threat for other travellers. After finishing their task, the men remounted their horses and the carriage once again left for its final destination.

27
Journey

They arrived at the gate a little over an hour later. The rain had died down. Shelter was far away and there had been no possibility to freshen up or even to change. Lily's dress had dried in several places leaving discoloured stains on her dress. Eliza had tried her best to fix her Mistress' hair, though wet, at least that looked presentable.

They were late, very late indeed. The weather had slowed them down considerably, and the delay at the pothole had done even more damage. Sir Marsh helped her out of the carriage. She thanked him, Eliza following her.

They entered the castle, escorted by guards. The men had been ordered to leave their weapons at the door; the horses had found safe shelter in the Palace stables.

John, the soldiers and Lieutenant Marsh were sent to a small building next to the kitchen. A room especially designed to fulfil the needs of travellers of lower ranks. They were the people who came to the capital for better work and living; the people the King never saw, as he did not converse outside the circles of nobility and high-ranking officers.

Lily fell into step next to Sir Marsh as they followed a servant down several corridors. Their wet shoes made ghastly noises on the floor. She tried to hide the stains on her dress, but almost giggled at the sight of Sir Marsh. He looked neither like a gentleman nor a soldier. He could have been mistaken for a peasant, if one looked no further than his soiled attire.

The servant opened the door to a grand hall where they would meet the representative of the King. Lily gasped. The hall was breathtaking with high ceilings, and walls filled with paintings and statues. She hardly knew where to look first, soon there was not enough time left to take everything in though, as a man she had not noticed yet stepped forward and stopped before them. He made a slight coughing sound, focusing their attention on him. He raised his eyebrows as he took in their appearance. Lily twiddled with her hands, unconsciously straightening her posture as the man's eyes glided over her.

'Sir, Milady, my name is Edward Faulkner, Duke of the providence Lina. I present the ladies to his majesty the King. I wonder though,' Again, he scrutinized her in a way that made her rather uncomfortable. She longed to turn away and leave. '.. if it's a good idea to present you as you are now.' He let the sentence linger in the air.

Lily did not know how to reply. 'The weather Sir…'

She hesitated. Sir Marsh picked up on her confusion and embarrassment.

'I assure you Sir; this young lady is a model of elegance and grace. I'm afraid the weather took a turn for the worse while we were travelling and we experienced some trouble underway. If you allow us some time to freshen up, you will see what I've had the pleasure to see since the first day we travelled together; her natural beauty, her propriety and manners. No doubt, you will be as charmed as every other person that had the privilege to ever become acquainted with her.'

Lily blushed at the overflow of compliments coming from the man standing next to her. She turned her gaze back to the Duke and gave a soft smile.

The Last Lord's Wife

Duke Faulkner examined her even more but said nothing for several minutes. He looked from one to the other and back again. They were standing close together, though careful not to touch, and from Sir Marsh's pose it was obvious he was protective of her. The Duke recounted his words. 'The weather has been very appalling indeed. If you follow Chester, he will show you to some rooms where you can freshen up. I will wait here for your return; I have some business to attend.'

Lily and Sir Marsh bowed and followed the servant out of the room.

Eliza still stood where they had left her, near the entrance to the hall. She quickly followed her mistress towards the grand stairs. Lily started to ascend the steps. She lifted her gown up with one hand and reached for the banister with the other, but failed to touch it soon enough. Her foot caught the hem of her dress, coming down with rapid movement on the slippery steps. Her shoes, still wet from the rain, gave her very little balance and she started to fall backwards. Sir Marsh caught her long before she could fall. The servant and Eliza were next to her in a heartbeat.

'Are you injured Milady?' it sounded from three sides.

Lily looked up to Sir Marsh and caught his eye; he had been deeply concerned for her wellbeing, as was evident from his longing look, careful placement of his hand on her back and his close proximity. She tried to straighten herself lest the servant would notice something between them.

'Yes, yes, I am fine.' She firmly grabbed the banister this time and leaned on it heavily. "I did not hurt myself, honestly. Let's not make anything out of this; it was just a clumsy moment.'

She smiled at them, though her heart raced in her chest, she gestured for them to continue. The servant turned and

Eliza, after giving her Mistress another lingering look, started to follow. Sir Marsh waited for Lily to go first. She turned to him and smiled, but her smile quickly turned to curiosity. Duke Faulkner was standing in the doorway, watching them with a questioning expression on his face. Lily pretended not to notice and followed the others upstairs. When they had cleared the stairs, she looked back, but the Duke was gone.

Eliza put the finishing touches on her Mistress' hair. Lilliane was clad in her best dress and after thoroughly scrubbing herself everywhere, not a trace of mud could now be seen. She had sat silently while Eliza prepared her to go back down. Eliza stood back and looked at her.

'You look beautiful Miss.' She noticed traces of tears on Lily's cheeks. 'You mustn't cry now Miss, it will only make you feel unhappy.'

Lily dried her tears with a handkerchief. She tried to smile at her maid, but failed miserably. Her sobbing worsened. 'I can not help it Eliza, I am losing him. I am already feeling wretched.' She dabbed her eyes again.

'I know Miss. I wish there was something I could say to make it all better.' Eliza comforted her as best she could. 'Is that handkerchief new Miss?' She asked, curiously looking at the white cloth.

Lily blushed, and handed it to her. It was white and was not decorated. In the corner the initials W.R.M. were visible. 'He gave it to me a few days ago. I guess I should return it; soon I will never see him again.'

Eliza gave it back, 'Keep it Miss, at least you can keep something of him close to your heart. It is a poor substitute, but it's something solid, something other than memories.' She stood, checking them both once more. 'We should go down, it will not get any easier, no matter how long we sit here.'

Lily nodded, and rose too. 'Yes, you are right. This is it; we can no longer avoid it.' She smiled poorly. 'How do I look?'

'Lovely Miss, I don't think I have ever seen you look more beautiful.'

'Let's go then.'

Eliza opened the door, and Lily, after taking a deep breath to try to relax herself, left the room.

The walk to the stairs was short. Lily paused at the top, slightly worried she might fall again. Her gaze fell on Sir Marsh, she smiled. He was standing at the bottom of the stairs in his best attire. He looked handsome like always, but she knew the smile on his face was only for her. She didn't think about falling again as she walked towards him. Their eyes remained locked the entire way down.

'You look beautiful Milady.'

'Thank you Sir, and may I say you look very handsome.'

'You may,' His smile faltered a moment, but he overcame it. 'Shall we?' Sir Marsh held out his hand for her to take. She tried not to think of where he was leading her; if she could hang on to this moment then nothing else mattered.

'Although I like this attire very much, you look just as beautiful covered with mud Milady.'

Lily stifled a laugh at that. Even as he led her back into the grand hall, she felt more relaxed near him than she had been up in the room.

They paused at the doorway. Sir Marsh turned towards her, his back facing part of the door. 'Milady, I..'

'Be silent, please.' Lily silenced him by placing her finger before his mouth. 'I know, believe me, I do, but I cannot bear to hear it right now. Please, for both our sakes, say no more.'

Sir Marsh nodded and said nothing else. Lily removed her hand, though the look she could not break. It was only when someone coughed next to them that they quickly moved away from each other. Duke Faulkner was standing only a few feet away. He said nothing, as he turned and went back inside. Lily and Sir Marsh followed him a few seconds later. The Duke had returned to were they had seen him stand before.

He coughed again. 'Sir, Milady, I had no doubt that this young lady was indeed the picture of gracefulness you described and I am honoured to say I was right. You are indeed very beautiful my dear.' He paused his speech. He looked as if he wanted to say more, so they kept quiet. Duke Faulkner paced a few steps before them. 'However, I am charged with finding the perfect bride for his Lordship the King. And I think…. I am of the opinion that you are not.'

'Are not... Sir?' Lily was stunned; had she heard him correctly?

'Yes Milady, you see, I'm an old romantic and when it comes to matters of the heart, I firmly believe you can only give it away once.' He winked at Lily. 'You are free to go. You have fulfilled your duty to our King to your best abilities and are welcome to return to your home.'

This time it was Sir Marsh who spoke first. 'Sir?' He looked at the Duke, conveying all he felt in his stare.

'Yes Sir, I am very serious.'

Sir Marsh faked a cough, hiding a deep sigh of relief.

He stuck out his hand for the Duke to shake. 'Thank you Sir, you have no idea what this means to us.'

'I have an inkling Sir.' Duke Faulkner bowed before Lily. 'Godspeed Milady.'

'And to you Sir.' Lily had trouble speaking as she was still trying to comprehend what was happening.

'I hope you fulfill your task,' said Sir Marsh.

'Oh, I will, I am very duty bound to it. It's a great honour for the King to entrust me. The servant will lead you to rooms if you wish to spend the night, for now, I must beg you to excuse me, my wife is waiting for me and tardiness is something she does not forgive easily.'

'I thank you Sir, but I think we prefer to travel onwards. Lady Lilliane has an aunt only a few miles away. She is eager to see her now that it is possible.'

'Very well, safe travels and better weather on your journey home.'

They both thanked him thoroughly, before following the same servant from earlier back outside. There was no time to talk as the servant led them directly to the rest of their party. Lily let Eliza fuss over her but did not utter one word about anything discussed. Sir Marsh ordered his men around. Before half an hour could pass, they were on the road again, this time the castle was only getting smaller.

They travelled to a town a few miles east from the capital. A town normally not on their route but now that Lily had the opportunity she was not going to pass it by. Mariah Price, her mother's other sister, and always a favourite with Lily and her brothers, resided there.

Her visits to Geastwood were sparse, as Louisa never enjoyed company much, not even her sister. It had been bittersweet to know her aunt was so near but not being able to visit; now it proved to be a blessing in disguise. Where else could a young maiden and her master of journey wait for instructions from her family now that their ultimate goal was no more?

Mrs Price greeted them with pure delight. Sir Marsh was led to his guest quarters as Lily was taken away by her aunt and showered with attention and love.

A letter was written and immediately sent off to her father, explaining the new situation and asking for his instructions. All they could do for now was wait.

Eliza opened the door for her mistress and followed her in quickly. She did not say a word as Lady Lilliane had barely said more than three words since leaving the castle.

She had trouble understanding what was going on, had they been dismissed, and if they had, why? Lady Lilliane was a charming and handsome young lady, yet if they weren't, why had they left the castle?

'I wish to change clothes Eliza, this gown is for special occasions.'

'Yes Miss.'

'And you may unpack half the trunk as we are unlikely to leave my aunt's house for several days now. It is fortunate indeed Aunt Price lives so close to the capital.'

Eliza obeyed immediately, offering very little correspondence as it was clear her mistress was deep in thought. She emptied their trunks and selected a simple blue gown. Lily was sitting on a chair, staring out the window, though she did not seem to see anything.

Eliza fiddled with her hands. 'Would you like to change now Miss, or would you prefer to wait? … Miss?' she tried again, as Lily made no response. Eliza placed her hand on her mistress' shoulder and jumped just as high as she did.

Lily put her hand on her heart. 'Oh, I'm sorry Eliza, I did not hear you, and I was in deep thought. What is it?'

'Your clothes are ready Miss.'

The Last Lord's Wife

'Yes, of course.' Lily rose, but remained quiet. She seemed to sink back into thought. Eliza helped her mistress change and redid her hair in the usual way she wore it. Kneeling down, Eliza tied her mistress' shoes.

'We were dismissed.'

It had come out in almost a whisper; Eliza had difficulty hearing it at first. She looked up to her mistress.

'Miss?'

Lily returned her stare. 'The representative of the King. He dismissed me of my duties. I am free.'

Eliza felt happiness grow inside her. 'Isn't that good news Miss? Now you are free to be with the one you love.'

Lily rose from the bed and started to pace the room. 'But what if he doesn't want me now? What if he only wanted me when I was attached to another?' She wrung her hands together.

'Miss.' Eliza stood, stopping before her and putting her hands on Lily's arms in an effort to calm her down. 'What did his Lordship give as his reason to dismiss you?'

'That you can only give your heart away once.'

'.. and if an unknown man like his Lordship can see that you love each other, surely it must be true. I have seen the looks Sir Marsh gives you when he thinks nobody is watching Milady. There is no doubt in my mind that you are the keeper of his heart.' Eliza let go of Lily and finished tidying things around the room. 'I may not know much Miss, but I know there can be no other truth than that.' When she looked back at her mistress, it was obvious Lily had rapidly calmed down. A light blush had appeared on her face.

'You know more than you realise Eliza.' Lily gave her maid a gentle squeeze. 'Thank you. You are right indeed. I know you are right.' She straightened herself and inhaled deeply. 'I

203

am ready to go downstairs.' Eliza opened the door for her, and Lily exited immediately.

Lily descended the stairs carefully. Her nerves were wreaking havoc on her insides and it took all her energy to appear calm. Eliza's encouragements had silenced her insecurities about Sir Marsh, but she could not be quite content with everything yet; it was not possible to understand the situation of being dismissed, therefore the mind could not be set to rest. She entered the drawing room, surprised to see Sir Marsh standing behind the table. He was alone, her aunt's voice came from somewhere at the back of the house. It was the first time they were without others since arriving. Lily hesitated only a moment.

'Oh my love.' He came to her in three easy strides and halted a mere foot away. His hand went up to her cheek, but he did not touch her.

'Could it really be true Sir? Am I free? Free from my obligation to the King?'

Tears glistened in her eyes as she waited for his reply. Sir Marsh held his breath while she spoke, but released it now. His grin was wider than she had ever seen it. She was sure her face mirrored his. Pure joy at hearing this wonderful news, yet a lingering doubt and shock. His lordship seemed genuine enough but what if it all turned out to be a cruel sort of joke? While that possibility remained, neither could really let go of their resolve to move on from each other. They said nothing, only stared at each other. Lily realised she no longer felt embarrassed by his poignant stare as no blush appeared on her cheeks. It delighted her fully. Before the echoes of a person coming towards them had faded away completely, they had moved apart.

Lily busied herself by pouring tea; Sir Marsh stared out of the window. A servant appeared and after bowing for them both, handed Sir Marsh a letter. He opened it and began to read in silence. Lily waited; inpatient to know what it held. She had recognised the King's grand zeal.

'Dear Sir,' Sir Marsh began to read with a steady voice. 'I am writing to inform you of the changes to your daughter's situation. As arranged by His Majesty our King. Your daughter came to the capital on the appointed date and offered herself as a potential bride for his Majesty. However, his majesty's choice fell on another. Your daughter is hereby released from her duty and free to return home.
May the Grace of our Lord be with you.
Yours truly,. Duke Faulkner.'

Sir Marsh looked at Lily. His entire face had lit up. She felt no shame as she catapulted herself into his arms. He swung her around once, before gently lowering her to the floor. His hold on her remained tight; she in turn snaked her arms around his neck. Without hesitation, their lips met, neither caring where they were or how improper it was.
'Lilliane,' Aunt's Price voice was filled with a mixture of shock and amusement. Sir Marsh released his grip on her and Lily quickly took a few steps back. They both blushed.
'I see there are some things you haven't told me yet. I look forward to hearing them. Now no more of that till your father has given his consent and things are more official.' Aunt Price smiled, then turned to Sir Marsh. 'Sir, your brother requests your expertise on a matter. He is waiting in the library. If you could be so kind to follow my servant, Bernard will show you where it is.'

Sir Marsh bowed his head, 'Yes, of course, thank you Milady.' He looked at Lily and winked, before leaving the room. Lily smiled.

Aunt Price took her hand and guided her to the sofa, they sat. 'I caught your mother once, kissing your father like that. She was so much in love with him. I remember when...'

Aunt Price started one of her stories. Though Lily was often quite amused with them, she had trouble keeping her focus now. Part of her was still relishing the feeling of being in his arms and hoped it wouldn't be long before she could be there again.

28

Trepidation

It was unimaginable and yet it was really happening; they were several days into travelling back to the castle where she had lived her entire childhood. Eliza sat next to her as the carriage carried them further away from the capital with every turn of the wheels. This time there had been no delays from sabotaged equipment or ambushes by thieves. Even the weather had been remarkably clear; a sure sign of warmer days approaching.

Earlier they had made an unannounced stop. The carriage had slowed to a halt and Sir Marsh, after opening the door, silently offered his hand. Lily did not hesitate in giving it. She instantly recognised the surrounding countryside. This was the spot where the saboteur had been revealed; the spot where Mr Johansson had killed her younger brother. Lily looked at Sir Marsh in question, but quickly realised his meaning as he led her to the graveside. Together they kneeled on the hill of Donovan's grave and prayed.

It had been a wet and gloomy day when the long awaited answer from her father finally arrived. It was short and to the point. Lily tried not to take it too personally, but had trouble blinking the tears away whenever she thought of it.

Sir Marsh,

> *I have just received your letter with the attached statement from our King's aid.*
> *The girl is expected back here as soon as it is possible.*
> *I will think of a new way to dispose of her.*
> *Greetings to you Sir,*
> *Lord F. Gaeli, Geastwood Castle.*

Lily held the letter in her hand, careful not to crumble it. Once again, there had been no message to her; there had barely been a civil word towards Sir Marsh. Lily attributed her father's attitude to the loss of Donovan. She had long ago buried the pain her parents caused her, their disinterest was evident, and never allowed herself to think about it very long. Sometimes it wasn't so simple though, the moments when clear evidence was presented to her; like this letter. She was glad to be alone. Aunt Price was off on a quick errand, and she had sent off Eliza. If her mother had been alive, it would have been different. Or would it have? Though she had few memories of her mother, they were all fond. She sighed; perhaps she was romanticizing everything.

Soft footsteps sounded in the hall outside the door. Steps she recognised as those belonging to Sir William Roderick Marsh. She waited, but heard nothing that suggested he had left or entered the room. From the feelings of warmth spreading through her body, she knew he was staring at her. Lily tried to smile, turning halfway to the door.

'My father's letter has arrived.'

Sir Marsh frowned at her tears, but did not speak. In three easy strives he was beside her and took the offered letter. Lily waited in silence while he read, watching his face intensely for signs of change. His earlier frown had turned into a scowl and she could clearly see anger beginning to rise. Their eyes met as soon as he finished the letter. With a finger, he softly wiped tears from her cheeks. It was all he could do at the moment. Both had sworn to Aunt Price to refrain from anything remotely intimate until things were settled properly. Servants were renowned for their talk and angry tongues could destroy a female's reputation in a heartbeat. Sir Marsh would be cast as a scoundrel as well.

'They clearly do not see how wonderful you are, and therefore are not worthy of you.'

Lily smiled at the compliment, dabbing the remainder of tears away with her handkerchief.

Sounds at the front door indicated the return of Aunt Price. Sir Marsh clicked his heels. 'Excuse me Milady.'

Nodding, Lily watched him leave. She could hear him exchange a few words with her aunt, followed by Aunt Price immediately coming into the room. 'Oh my dear girl. What sorrows we must endure in our lives and sometimes so much at the same time.'

Mrs Price enfolded Lily in her arms and pressed her to her chest. 'As young as you are, I am deeply impressed with how you handle things. I do not know a person twice your age that could do it any better.'

'Thank you Aunt,' Lily replied, returning the hug fully.

She stayed in her aunt's arms for several more minutes, letting her fuss over her like a mother would, all the while silently sending a thank you to Sir Marsh. He had made sure someone was giving her the comfort she needed, while he couldn't provide it himself.

She loved him dearly for it.

They had passed the halfway mark several miles back, a small town that barely held more than a handful of peasants. Dusk was vastly approaching but the carriage with its precious cargo and company was still riding at maximum speed. The castle was near, so close in fact that Lily slowly recognised bits of the countryside around her.

Her spirits were elevated. Many hours she spent conversing with Eliza. They spoke of times passed and of Beth, mother to Eliza and Lily's childhood nurse. Both were enjoying themselves. Lily even tried to touch upon the subject of Mr Johansson and her role in it all, but the girl, either from unwillingness to bring back bad memories or from simply not having a memory at all, soon fell silent on the subject.

Talk of the future was successfully avoided; without her father's consent Lily knew not if she was permitted to be with Sir Marsh. It was a matter that she, for the time being, buried deep inside herself

Seeing the outskirts of the park and stream leading to the castle brought a silence over the pair like nothing else could have done. Lily's eyes filled with tears; seeing everything again had been something she dearly desired, but had been sure it would not happen, at least not any time soon. To be back at her home now was a blessing. Next to her Eliza mirrored her smile. It would not be long now before she was truly home; back at Castle Geastwood.

She knew not what to expect. Presuming from the letter, her return would not be celebrated, she did not think an entire party would be waiting for their arrival. The sole henchman on the square had left the moment they had come in view of each other and it was several more minutes before someone else came out to greet them. It was Aunt Louisa herself; her face bearing no joy or agreement. There had been no plans for returning and Aunt Louisa had never been one for sudden inconsistencies in her arrangements. Judging from her aunt's expression, her return was not regarded in the manner that her departure had been.

Lily exited the carriage, keeping her expression neutral. Sir Marsh was standing nearby next to his horse but he offered no assistance. They had agreed a certain amount of distance was necessary before her father could be asked for his consent.

Aunt Louisa was clearly agitated. She grabbed Lily's arms painfully and proceeded to shake her. 'Why did you come back? And what happened to my son? My son.'

'Madame, please contain yourself.' Sir Marsh quickly stepped towards them.

Lily knew silence was the only answer her aunt would be satisfied with when enraged, Sir Marsh however was not as familiar with her aunt's moods and proceeded to tell her off until the shaking came to a halt.

Lady Louisa turned to Sir Marsh and tried to smile. 'I apologize Sir; I know this is not the time or place. Grief overcame me for a moment. If you follow my man, he will bring you to where you can freshen up. Lady Lilliane's father is eager to see her. He will send for you after.'

Sir Marsh looked at Lily, unsure of what to do. She nodded in encouragement. Often her aunt's moods would settle down as quick as they rose. Their party retreated inside as belongings and horses were squared away by servants and soldiers. Eliza had permission to see her family. Sir Marsh had gone inside as well.

Lily followed her aunt in another direction, alone.

Lily trailed her into a remote section of the castle, which was used very seldom. Her aunt was rapidly making her way through the corridors. Lily had trouble keeping up as she did not want to run. Neither had spoken a word since leaving the others. Aunt Louisa, mostly mumbling incoherently to herself, had barely glanced back at her. Lily knew what her aunt expected of her and resolved to keep silent until she was spoken to.

The corridor ended at a battered old door that Lily knew led to a tower room that was not used by anyone except Aunt Louisa. It was her own personal space that no other except her lady's maid entered without Lady Louisa. Melanie was the only person permitted to clean. The rest of the personnel, people who had served the family their whole lives, as their fathers and mothers before them, avoided this tower as if entering it would be punishable by death.

Lily had only been there once or twice before; when something she had done had irked Aunt Louisa so much that strict punishment was deemed necessary.

Lily did not have any fond memories of that place, yet she did not hesitate in following her aunt up the circular stairs. Her duties as a niece and stepdaughter had always been perfectly clear. Obey without question; follow without hesitation and never ever object. She knew the stairs were long, but her aunt was taking the steps at a tremendous speed. She was obviously in a hurry to go up. The door closed behind Lily with a bang. Lily froze on the spot. The room was as she remembered, a little dustier perhaps which was evidence that even Aunt Louisa's maid was not allowed here anymore. Lily often wondered why her father put up with such eccentrics. He who strived to be proper in every way could not have wed a stranger creature in Aunt Louisa, but then she had always attributed her being

Lady Lilliane's sister and living with them when her mother was murdered, the main reason for her father marrying her. She very much doubted him having any affection for her. Her father needed an heir, and Louisa had given him two.

Lady Louisa stared out the window for several minutes without speaking. Her body was rapidly going up and down as if in severe pain or distress. Lily hesitated, then decided to move forward and gently placed her hand on her aunt's shoulder. Lady Louisa spun on the spot, glaring at Lily full out. Lily could now clearly read from the expression on her face that it was rage and nothing else that had moved her upstairs so fast, though what could have angered her to such a level was beyond compression at the moment. Surely grief over her brother and not anger over the situation would be the primary emotion present at the castle.

'*You*,' was the only word Lady Louisa uttered.

'Milady?'

'Why couldn't they have killed you? Why did you have to kill my son, my son.'

'Mother, I did not kill your son, he was killed by a horrible man, a viper conspiring against us. He died in my arms. I would have given my own life to save him, but he had been wounded so severely that he passed within minutes.' Lily brushed away the tears at this admission. 'I assure you, we did all we could.'

The elder woman shook off Lily's hand. 'Why should I believe you, you have been nothing but trouble for me.' Her voice lowered to a hiss. 'Devil's child,' she uttered almost at a whisper, 'Devil's child.'

Lily was shocked to see her aunt this way; she had never acted this strange before, it was almost maniacal behaviour. Lady Louisa was starting to scare her. She took half a step towards the door. 'Perhaps we should go to Father, he is expecting us. Some tea will do you good Mother.'

'Don't call me mother.' Lady Louisa slapped Lily across the face. 'You are nothing to me, you are like her; evil. You took him away from me.' Stepping away from Lily, she started to walk around, kneading her hands in a repeated motion. 'You never wanted me to have him either; you made sure they took him away from me. All I wanted was to keep him, love him, but you wouldn't let me and now you send her to finish it.'

Lily wasn't sure if her aunt was talking to her or even who she was speaking about. She was hesitant on whether to leave and get help. Aunt Louisa was acting very peculiar 'Who took him Aunt?' she offered softly, hoping a simple question could get a rational answer.

Her aunt immediately turned her eye on Lily and glared. 'You know who I mean,' she hissed through her teeth. 'She took my son, my son.'

'Donovan was shot by a man, there was no female who took him.'

Aunt Louisa let out a low growl in her throat. 'Do you not know what I'm talking about? Are you not in on it. I am not talking about the boy.' She stopped shouting and turned her head away, towards the sole window. 'It's a shame about the boy.' Her voice had gone so soft Lily had trouble hearing her, but her words were making even less sense than before. Her aunt's behaviour was very disturbing. 'Yes, it's a shame about the boy. Still... all I ever wanted was my son, my first son. I loved him so much and she took him away.'

Lily was growing more confused by the minute, in an effort to break her aunt from her incoherent rambling, she went to touch her again, but before she could Aunt Louisa had suddenly turned and slapped Lily's across the face twice. Lily stood momentarily still from the blow.

'Don't you touch me; now tell me where he is? Where is my James?'

'I don't know anyone named James, Aunt... .' Lily paused, 'except for... Mr Johansson. He was your son?'

Aunt Louisa's face was clear as day; Lily had guessed correctly. She took a step back, turning it over in her mind. 'If James Johansson was your son and Donovan... then Mr Johansson killed his own brother. Did he know Donovan was his brother? Is that why he killed himself? But you were never married before Father.' Lily had paced the room while she fired question after question. Lady Louisa did nothing but stare. 'Aunt Louisa, who was the woman who took your son away from you?' She swallowed, gathering courage. 'Was it my mother?'

Again, Aunt Louisa did not reply in words; instead she raised her arm upwards. Lily saw something glistening in her hand and recognised it immediately. Fear washed over her. She knew she had been right again.

29
Aid

Sir Marsh paced the room with powerful strides. It was the same room he had occupied last time; he smiled as he remembered Lady Lilliane walking in on him in a rather compromising position. She had intrigued him from the start. Most ladies were always as proper as can be, but Lily did not pretend to be anything. Her sharp tongue made him wince at times, on other occasions it made him smile. Mostly he admired her kindness and compassion.

He had tried to distract himself by thinking of places he would take her if they were permitted to wed, but his worry grew with every minute that passed. Though he did not know how or why, he knew that Lily was in danger.

Grabbing his coat, he left the room. In the corridor he nearly bumped into Eliza. He tipped his head, distracted.

'Excuse me Sir. Have you seen Lady Lilliane? I can not find her; her father is asking for her.'

Sir Marsh sucked in his breath. 'I knew something was wrong. Eliza, perhaps you can tell me if Lady Louisa has a specific chamber she inhabits often?'

'She does Sir. I will take you there now.'

Sir Marsh nodded, 'We should hurry. I did not care for the look in her eye.'

'If I may be so bold Sir,' replied Eliza, '…. neither did I.'

Lily reacted on instinct. Her body flew sideways to the floor as the dagger was thrown towards her. The blade was familiar though, she had only seen it once before, more than a decade ago. Unsure of what was happening; she didn't get up right away, which gave Aunt Louisa time to retract the dagger. She put it away, out of sight.

'Get up from the floor, you're not an animal.'

It was said in a non-conversant tone and Lily obeyed as if her aunt had not just sent a weapon towards her.

'That's …. That is what killed my mother. I remember, the form, the colour, how…' She strained to regain control. 'how did you get it?'

Aunt Louisa laughed hysterically. 'I had to rid myself of the evil that stole my son.' She smirked, 'I did you a favour.'

'A favour? A favour.' Lily's voice was shrill. Her aunt's choice of words made anger rise inside her. She felt herself on the verge of exploding. 'You murdered my mother. You took away the only person that truly loved me. And for what? Because you blamed her for something that you can't even prove she did.'

'Can not prove? She told me I couldn't keep my child because I was not wed; she said I was disgracing our family with my wild behaviour.' Lady Louisa stepped so close Lily could feel her hot breath on her face. She poked the girl in the chest with her finger. 'And then I had to watch her give my child to someone else, I was helpless to do anything. Soon after that, she had you and she flaunted you in my face. You were her precious little girl, her darling gift from the heavens. I saw what you really were though; a devil's child; evil, just like her. I knew it was my duty to rid the world of such an evil, and that is just what I tried to do that day, that is all. '

Aunt Louisa placed her hand on Lily's arm in such a loving gesture that it made Lily uncomfortable, she could barely remember the last time she had been so sweet. The desire to know the absolute truth was overpowering and the only thing keeping her from running out and telling all to her father.

'Can you really blame me?' Her voice was pleading, yet Lily did not dare to reply to the underlying question, for fear of losing self-control.

'Tell me everything.' Lily was curt, but resolute.

Aunt Louisa nodded. She released her grip on Lily's arm and started to pace again. 'I planned to kill you first, then my sister. That way it would seem as if she had gone mad and killed you.

I had taken you away from your nurse. I told Beth I was going for a walk. She obeyed but I think she may have told your mother because we were followed sooner than I had expected. I had the dagger out. Lilliane came and saw it. She ran towards me and I stabbed her. It was self-defence really. She wanted to hurt me, that's why she ran towards me.' She looked back at Lily. 'Wouldn't you have done the same if you were in my situation?'

'I would never be in your situation Aunt.'

The saddened look on her aunt's face melted away instantly at that reply and rage once again took over. Aunt Louisa lifted her arm; the dagger gleamed in the afternoon light coming from the window. Lily raised her hands to protect herself as Aunt Louisa charged at her.

Lily quickly retreated until the cold, stone wall against her back told her that there was no escape possible. Fearfully, she saw the gleaming blade come down full force as her aunt had followed her closely. With a force she did not know she possessed, she clamped her hands around her aunt's arm, trying to keep the knife from reaching her chest. Her arms were trembling with the effort and Lily knew this wasn't a fight she was going to win if she didn't distract her aunt and kept her talking. 'Why didn't you kill me right after you'd killed my mother? Why wait all these years?'

Her aunt grunted from the strain of trying the push the dagger forward. 'Your father, he would have realised my guilt. I liked living here too much, I had nowhere else to go, putting up with you was almost worth it, but I did my best to get rid of you as soon as I could.' Aunt Louisa tried to push Lily's hands down with her free hand. 'You should have stayed away.'

Tears began to prickle in her eyes as desperation started to take over. 'Please, Aunt Louisa, that's what I came to tell my father. I'm leaving the castle; Sir Marsh has asked me to marry him. Please, let me go and you will never see me again.'

'Do you think I'm an idiot, little girl?' Aunt Louisa screeched and wrapped her hand tightly around Lily's throat. 'Do you think that I don't know that you will go running to your father the minute I let you leave? You will ruin everything I've worked so hard for and what's more, you will get to have your happily ever after, while my dear boy lies cold in the ground.' Lady Louisa's eyes were bulging and her voice rose another pitch. 'Do you think that I will let you live the life my son deserved to have, that I will let you and Sir Marsh be happy together?'

Lily's reply was lost as the door flew open. Both females looked up and Lily took the opportunity to push her aunt away, however her aunt's grip on her throat did not loosen. The fresher air on her back told her Lady Louisa was moving her towards the window. She knew that the fall would kill her.

'Let her go.' The sound of Sir Marsh's voice filled her with renewed strength to fight back. She twisted and turned her body until her aunt could no longer keep her grip on both Lily and the dagger, letting go of the former, to fully grip the latter with both hands.

Yet the arrival of others had not lessened her aunt's anger; in fact, it seemed to work as an incentive to finish what she had started quicker. Lady Louisa slammed Lily into the wall; Lily could feel the window sill digging in her back. She knew she would soon lose her remaining balance and topple backwards out of the tower. Her aunt's strength was pushing her towards the back and she could feel her own slipping away. Perhaps she had hallucinated Sir Marsh's voice as it was obvious that nobody was helping her. In her last moments, she could only think about her poor mother; murdered by her own sister; and what a horrible death falling down must be.

She closed her eyes as her foot slipped and the last bit of balance left her. For a brief moment, there was nothing but air around her, until hands fastened around her arms. They were nothing like before, though firmer than her aunt's they were also as gentle as could be. Lily opened her eyes, surprised that the screams she had been hearing had not been coming from her own lips. Eliza and Sir Marsh were pulling her away from the window. The dagger had fallen to the floor, its owner nowhere visible.

'Are you alright Milady?'

She had no answer for them. Eliza was making sure her mistress was not fatally wounded anywhere and Sir Marsh still had not let go of her arm.

'Where is she?' asked Lily, finding it difficult to speak.

Eliza did not respond; Sir Marsh only looked at the window. Carefully Lily walked back, unaware that the other two were shadowing her closely. She glanced out the window long enough to make sure. A crowd was already forming around

The Last Lord's Wife

the body of her aunt and she knew it would not be long before her father would know.

Eliza had finished, she felt satisfied her mistress would be better soon. 'Only a few cuts and scrapes Miss, you were lucky.'

Lily retreated from the window once more. The room was beginning to suffocate her.

'It's over now Milady.' Sir Marsh's voice was soft and gentle.

Lily nodded in response, only to suddenly stand from the seat she had been pushed in to moments before.

'No, it's not over. Not yet, first I have to see my father.' Lily suddenly felt determined and left through the door down the stairs, followed close behind by the two that had saved her life.

When Lily stopped in the corridor leading to her father's chambers, she realised that she had basically ran there all the way without stopping. Even the pace that her aunt had used to climb up the tower had been nothing compared to the speed Lily had adopted. She was vaguely aware of the two people following her, as they spoke in hushed tones to each other, but did not comprehend any of their words, or even what their primary feeling was at present.

Her breath was coming out in rapid movements and her heart was pounding around in her chest. She felt no pain or fear at the moment, no grief over her aunt's confessions or behaviour. The urge to see her father nearly overwhelmed her and drowned out all other feeling.

She could not imagine her father being aware of his wife's devious manners, and even when that inkling had entered her mind; it only took mere seconds for it to be dismissed. Her father, though aloof at times and not very interested in his only daughter's future or present of mind, was never cruel, never spiteful like her aunt had been many times.

She reached the outer chambers of his room and begged the servant there for an entry. He curtsied quietly and exited to make her presence known to his master. She had always liked that man. He was gentle in his manners and kindness was second nature.

A quiet cough behind her told she wasn't alone; she turned to see Sir Marsh and Eliza. Only now did she truly register Eliza's coloured cheeks and shallow breathing, evidence that they had followed her here, matching her speed. Even Sir Marsh needed a moment to collect himself. She held back a smile; her speed had truly been exceptional.

'I'm sorry I didn't wait for you.'

Sir Marsh grinned, taking the cup of liquid a servant offered him.

'You run very fast Miss,' Eliza said, smiling.

'Thank you,' she said, 'I shall go in to speak to my father now.'

Eliza made no objection, as her mistress wishes always went before her own, but Sir Marsh could not help but gently place his hand on her arm.

'Miss Lily?'

Lily stopped him from following her further. 'Wait please; I think I need to do this alone.'

'Are you sure?'

Lily smiled to reassure him. 'He's my father. He does not mean me harm, he never has. There is only one other person in the world I trust more.' She didn't elaborate further, but there was no need.

He grinned bashfully, before nodding and released her arm. 'Eliza and I will wait here.' Sir Marsh looked at Eliza's cheeks which were still flushed from the exercise. 'I shall make sure she has some refreshments.'

Lily flashes a grin back, before taking a deep sigh and turning serious again. The servant opened the door for her and she entered her father's chambers.

It had been a long time since her last visit. She could easily distinguish all the changes in the scenery, but none were as grand as the alterations in her father. The change in atmosphere was clear from the moment she entered. Her father was facing away from her, his shoulders were down and his body was rigid. The change in his stance was evident and it frightened her. He had always seemed so strong to her. Beyond reproach even, but his second wife's betrayal had obviously taken its toll on him...

'Father?' She nearly whispered. Her tone was so soft she wasn't sure he had heard her at first, until his body stiffened even more. It was only a few steps towards him, and she made them without hesitation. She was not scared of this man, she couldn't be.

Gently she placed her hand on his arm. He turned swiftly and she was surprised, shocked even, to see tears glistening on his cheeks.

'Oh Father,' was all she said, before throwing her arms around his waist. She felt the tears come at last, earlier she had concentrated her whole being on reaching her father, for fear of breaking down from recent events, now that was no longer necessary. Her body shook in time with his. Several minutes passed before either said anything. At last the flow of liquid from both pair of eyes came to a halt. She looked up to his face as he began to speak, loosening her hold on him.

'I am so sorry, my dear child.' He had trouble forming the words, even as he regained some of his composure.

'It's not your fault Father. She fooled us all, for many years.'

Lord Frederick nodded, but it was not done with great conviction. 'I keep thinking about my poor boy, I should have never let either of you go on this journey. My poor Donovan, dead; did he suffer?'

'No Father, it was very quick.'

Lord Frederick nodded slowly, lifting his eyes to Lily for the first time since she had entered the room. He smiled sadly.

'And you, my daughter, how have you been? Did you suffer at all?'

'Sir Marsh took very good care of me Father.'

'Good.'

Her father nodded curtly and for a moment Lily saw some of his bravery return, but it didn't last long. The grief his wife had done him and the death of his son had aged him considerably. He looked older than she had ever seen him.

'What are your plans now?'

His question surprised her, catching her off guard. She stumbled for a quick answer.

'Whatever you plan for me Sir.'

Lord Frederick patted her hand.

'Dear girl, good daughter. I would not have expected another answer from you, but I permit you to be honest. I think we owe that to each other.'

Lily gazed at her father for a long moment before placing her hand on top of her father's and squeezing it.

'I want to marry him Father. I love him and he loves me, deeply.'

Lord Frederick caressed her cheek with his free hand. 'Marsh?'

Lily nodded.

'Then that is what shall happen.'

Lord's Frederick's smile was genuine and heartfelt. Lily hugged her father again, this time he returned the gesture fully. They talked for a moment longer, before Lily was dismissed. She exited her father's chamber with a bounce in her steps that had not been there before. Sir Marsh's eye was the first that caught hers. She smiled, nodding slowly. He let out a breath he had been holding and his body physically relaxed. Lily stopped only a foot away from him. 'My father wishes to speak to you now Sir, if it is at your convenience.'

Sir Marsh rose from his seat and clicked his heels. 'Of course Milady, I beg you to excuse me.' As he brushed past her, she did not miss the soft tap he gave her hand.

Lily turned to Eliza. They started to walk towards the main corridor. Her pace was much slower this time. The events of the day had finally started to catch up with her. She felt drained, and very tired, but happy as well. Her rooms had been prepared for her, as were guest chambers for the others. Eliza followed her as they entered her rooms. The girl bustled around her but Lily barely noticed. She was asleep as soon as her head hit the pillow.

30
Finale

The castle had been in mourning since the unfortunate passing of its primary heir. Yet Lord Frederick, his lady and the last remaining child, young master Frederick, had still held their dinners together, albeit in a more subdued manner than usual. The news of Lady Louisa's death spread through the surroundings within the hour, with many an innuendo about the circumstances preceding her fall. Some servants had seen the young Miss Lilliane with her maid and a gentleman leave from the general vicinity of the tower, but nobody had any direct knowledge. Eliza never gossiped and it was sure that the gentleman and lady would keep as silent as the grave. His Lordship did not leave his chambers at all that afternoon and none of the others dined in the large dining room either. Miss Lilliane was seen wandering around the corridors, accompanied by her maid. The gentleman remained in conversation within Lord Frederick's chambers. Though the staff's curiosity was peaked they continued their work as meticulously as if Lady Louisa was still watching over their shoulders.

Lily paced the same corridor a second time. She was anxious for Sir Marsh to exit her father's room. He seemed to take an eternity to come out. Eliza watched her mistress with a small knowing smile playing on her lips.

Lily looked at her maid. 'Eliza.'

'I didn't say anything Miss.'

'Just don't smile at my expense.'

Eliza tried hard not to burst out in laughing at that. 'I wouldn't dream of it Miss.'

Despite of her anxiety, Lily smiled at that. 'He's been taking a long time.'

'It's only been three hours, you were asleep for nearly two Milady.'

'You don't find three hours a long time?'

'You were in with your father for two hours yourself this morning.'

Lily looked at Eliza in question. 'I was? Surely it was less than that.'

'It was indeed two hours Miss. His Lordship's manservant assured me of it.' Eliza took a step forward before Lily could start pacing again. 'Why don't we take some refreshments on the balcony? I'm sure Sir Marsh will join us as soon as he has finished his business with your father.'

Nodding, Lily started to walk into the right direction. 'Yes, I'm sure you are right Eliza, all I'm doing now is wearing holes in the carpet.'

Eliza followed her with a larger grin on her face.

'Stop smiling Eliza.' Lily said, not turning towards her. Eliza giggled softly in return.

Sir Marsh closed the door behind him, feeling rather pleased with the conclusion of the conversation. He wanted nothing more than to run to Lady Lilliane and tell her everything, but decorum dictated he keep his composure and walk the length of the hallway at a steady pace. After following directions from a servant, he found Lily sitting with Eliza in a parlour that was opened up entirely on one side to let in fresh air. It opened to a huge balcony overseeing the whole courtyard.

The bustle of the daily life in the castle floated towards them from below.

Sir Marsh took a moment to look at Lily. This was her place of birth, where she had spent her childhood. She was in her element here. He had never seen her this comfortable with herself. When he had first met her, he had not noticed the little things, too overwhelmed with her as a person to look further. Here familiarity surrounded her; she knew each person by name, could talk to them with ease. Any problem she could solve and she did everything with a gentle hand and an encouraging smile. He was never more proud of her. Only when Eliza looked directly at him and curtsied did he move away from the door. He felt he could have stood there for days, content in watching Lily.

Lily's smile grew deeper when Sir Marsh took the seat beside her. She had felt his arrival several minutes before, but had not acknowledged anything, as he was not coming forward. Eliza felt no such discretion. Lily was pleased to see him in a good mood after returning from his confinement with her father. She nodded in acknowledgement as he took the seat beside her wordlessly.

Sir Marsh looked at the people busying around the courtyard, she followed his gaze. 'Your father expressed wishes to hold a memorial for Donovan. I persuaded him to include your aunt in that too. However little I cared for her, it is best for him not to lose too much face among his countrymen. I hope you do not find me improper here.'

'No, indeed,' Lily answered, even as she adjusted the scarf around the marks her aunt had left on her neck. 'Father must not suffer more from his foolish wife. We've all made choices that turned out to be wrong in the end. And for all her faults she still did one thing right.' Lily pointed at a fine looking young man visible in the courtyard. It was clear that the people admired and respected him, even for his young age. 'My brother Frederick will honour his father and brother properly. He will take care that everyone is well provided for.' She looked at Sir Marsh and smiled. 'I'm inclined to focus on my love for him and not on my hatred for Lady Louisa.'

They sat in silence till Eliza came back over to them with refreshments. Lily had not noticed her leaving. She served them tea and biscuits, then left.

'There are certain disadvantages to taking anyone as a wife.' Lily was the first to break through the silence.

Sir Marsh's curiosity peeked at that. 'Why do you say that?'

'Because you never really know a person, do they even know themselves? You may be attracted to each other in the beginning, but who is to say it won't go horribly wrong. I'm sure my father never imagined having to bury two wives.'

'Who is to say it won't be a good life together. And if you don't make that choice, but rather stay alone your entire life, it might be horribly wrong that way. Tempers can be strong, but there must be genuine reason that you fell for each other in the first place. I exclude unions based on wealth, status or convenience of course. I'm talking marriages of equals. If you fall in love with somebody and there are no reasons against a union, why should you not wed? My mother and father were very happy together; as I am sure yours were as well. Your father told me how much he loved your mother, and that even marriage to Lady Louisa was not all unpleasant in the beginning. I'm rather of the opinion that any gentleman capable should try to wed.' He looked at Lilliane as he ended his speech and saw a grin on her lips. 'Forgive me, I spoke out of bounds.'

'Not at all, I can see that you are passionate about the subject, as you should be, since you are, in fact, a gentleman capable of marriage.'

'And you, as a lady?'

'For a lady it's often more a necessity, a duty, than a want or need. Society is not very gentle to ladies who do not wed. From infancy we are told that we must marry, and that we must marry well.'

'And if you were to marry me?'

'If I would have had to marry his Majesty it would have been a duty, but I marry you because it is the thing I want most in the world. Do you still want to marry me, after seeing such madness in my family?'

'I would marry you even if you were mad.' Sir Marsh winked, making Lily giggle.

After a moment she went back to being serious. 'She killed my mother.'

'Yes.'

'Because my mother took her child away.'

'Your mother was doing what was right for your family.'

'But was it right for my aunt? Or her child? The child that ended up killing his brother.'

'It is difficult to judge such situations when not faced with them directly.'

Lily nodded in afterthought. 'True. And who knows what would have happened if my mother had lived; we may have never met.'

Sir Marsh took her hands in his own, looking directly into her eyes. 'I would rather not consider that.'

Returning his look, Lily smiled genuinely. 'Me neither.'

A period of mourning followed the ceremony for Donovan and his mother that threw a small dark cloud over their engagement, but the courting was still enjoyed by both. Invitations were send out to family members and intimate acquaintances by order of Lord Frederick himself. He was making arrangements for a large celebration. Lily protested heartily to everything she found too extravagant but it fell on deaf ears with her father, and Sir Marsh was not helping either; he delighted in every proposal her father brought forward, no matter how ludicrous it seemed. It brought some anxiety for Lily that the men did not have. At last the week arrived and the excitement grew for all involved.

Guests arrived nearly every hour. They spent most of the time giving introductions and paying respects to those unacquainted for a long time. Lily could see Sir Marsh was not always keeping his attentions on who he was conversing with at that time, though she doubted anyone else noticed it. He was keeping an eye out for a certain carriage he knew well.

An invite to the ceremony and all the celebrations surrounding it had gone out to his mother as soon as the date was sure, and an equally rapid answer had been received in reply, but so far they had not arrived yet. Sir Marsh was successful in keeping up appearances until a lone servant singled him out with a letter that appeared to be delivered only a moment ago. Lily watched as he opened it and his facial expression changed to neutral. He looked up and met her eye, a small smile returned when he noticed she had been watching him. She quickly excused herself and left for a more private corner of the room. He was doing the same.

The letter he gave her was only one sheet, but there seemed to be much more in the envelope. He said nothing about that and she focused her attention on the letter at hand.

> *My darling son William,*
>
> *I am sorrier than you will understand, until you have children of your own that is, to have to write this letter. I'm afraid your sister Cathy and I are unable to attend your nuptials.*
>
> *Cathy has caught a violent cold three days ago, I was praying it would get better soon, but I'm afraid her health has not improved yet to the point of making the journey towards you. Do not fear for her, though she is ill, it is not life threatening. I shall dearly regret missing your wedding each day my son, but I cannot leave Cathy at this moment. Your brother John shall have to do as your family attending. I hope you and Lady Lilliane will visit us soon. I, as well as Cathy, am eager to acquaint Lady Lilliane better.*
>
> *Joy and happiness are my wishes for the journey you are about to start. Your choice for a wife is exactly what I always pictured for you. I must close now; your sister is in need of me.*
>
> *Yours sincerely,*
> *Catherine Marsh.*

As she finished reading Lily looked up to catch his eye. He smiled back poorly.

'I was afraid something like this would happen. I suppose I should be happy my brother is here. He will indeed have to do as my family.'

'And me,' added Lily.

'Yes, and you, but you're not just my family, you're my everything.'

They shared another smile, but their surroundings kept them from continuing the conversation. Lord Frederick was already coming towards them, followed by several new arrivals. Lily gave back the letter, and started to turn towards her father.

'Wait, my mother sends this letter.' He handed her the envelope and put his own letter in a pocket. 'It's addressed to you, I did not read it.'

Surprised, Lily took it, but there was no time to read it, as at that moment her father required her full attention.

The ladies took leave later in the afternoon, Lily among them. It was the first opportunity she had to seclude herself; and she grabbed it with both hands. As soon as the door to her chambers closed, she took out the envelope and sat down to read its contents.

> *Dear Lady Lilliane,*
>
> *Firstly, I would like to congratulate you most sincerely regarding your engagement with my son William. Words can hardly express how happy I am at the prospect of you becoming my daughter. I could see how much William loved you by the way he treated you.*
>
> *I hope you will not find me discourteous, I know our acquaintance was rather short, and then for me to write a letter like this... I would have told you this in person, if I had been capable of coming, but I expect my son has told you why I am unable to.*
>
> *When I visited your group some time ago, before the untimely death of your brother; my deepest condolences on that, I took two liberties*

that I normally would not take so easily with anyone.

First, I asked to talk to your lady's maid. Second, I talked to you about my son John in a rather intimate way. I did this for various reasons, which, now that it is known who was working against you while travelling, I can disclose fully. I hope you will permit an old lady some lenience.

My sons are, as I told you in our previous conversation, very different. William, and Edmund, have always been open and cheerful. John has a much more solemn nature, not quick to act, but when he does, it is often perceived as odd to people who are not intimately acquainted with him. I often tried to get him to open up more, but it was never in his disposition.

When William first shared his suspicions about a saboteur amongst your group, I, shamefully admit, could not be sure of my youngest son's involvement. As his mother I know I should never question his honour. I conversed with your servant and soon found she knew nothing more than what she told you and William. Her memory was truly gone, and nothing in her manner implicated my John. Knowing from William's letter, and his manner in your presence that he cared deeply for you, I instead decided to focus on trying to acquaint you and John better. For William, and the rest of our family. We are very small now, and need to be there for each other. I pray you will keep this to yourself.

> *Now you know all my reasons for my behaviour last time. I hope it clears up any lingering questions you had. I find it important to start a new life with a clean slate and, perhaps even more important, a clean conscience. Though my methods may not always be what society calls regular, my intentions are always for the good of my family. My entire family, which I welcome you to with open arms. I must close now, Cathy needs me.*
> *Kind regards,*
> *Catherine Marsh.*

Lily held the letter in her hand and studied the penmanship. She now knew why Mrs Marsh had wanted to see Eliza in private, a servant she had never met before. Finding out others had often thought of John Marsh as odd eased her mind with regard to her own behaviour on that matter. She had regularly chastised herself for her prejudgement against him. They were getting better acquainted each day. He was much more forthcoming after telling her about his illness and was thankful she helped him tell his brother.

Lily decided to keep some parts of the letter to herself to spare either brother any suffering, but would share some of the highlights with Sir Marsh. He would soon be her husband after all and her most beloved confidante.

The letter was tucked away safely with other keepsakes, though not before it was read twice more. Lily marvelled how well Mrs Marsh seemed to know her sons, was saddened to never have met Edmund and Mr Marsh personally and felt eager to get better acquainted with Mrs Marsh and the little girl. She doubted that life with this family would ever be dull.

She rose before Eliza knocked on the door. The last hour was spent pondering about the future and what it might bring. Excitement and anxiety fought to control her mood. How quickly everything had changed in such a short time.

Eliza laid out the dress she would wear today; her mother's wedding gown, modernized and adjusted to fit her. The shoes were already cleaned and glimmering. Eliza had once again outdone herself.

'Shall I help you dress Miss?' Eliza asked tenderly.

Lily nodded and took the required position. Eliza smiled. 'Nervous Miss?'

'Yes, but also…' She paused, looking for the right word.

'Happy.' Eliza finished for her.

'Exactly, very happy.'

'I'm glad Miss. He suits you well, and such a handsome man too. We shall have you ready in a jiffy, to walk down that aisle.'

Lily's large grin was enough of a response for Eliza, and she busied about preparing her mistress for her wedding day. It wasn't long before a servant came to collect them and the service began.

One look at Sir Marsh was all that was necessary to dissipate her nerves. All she was left with was pure happiness. They never looked away as she walked towards him.

The ceremony began, first with a few words from her father, and then continued by the priest. Throughout the nuptials Lily kept her excitement in check. Sir Marsh however had the happiest of looks on his face, which only seemed to grow whenever he caught her eye. Before the hour was over, she had become Lady Lilliane Marsh, a Lord's wife.

CPSIA information can be obtained at www.ICGtesting.com
Printed in the USA
BVOW03s1407290414

352044BV00001B/56/P